THE
BOMBERS'
MOON

Betty Vander Els

FARRAR · STRAUS · GIROUX

NEW YORK

For Barth,
Jonathan, Nat, Mia, and Alix
with all my love—

and to Mary Cash, my editor

The Bombers' Moon

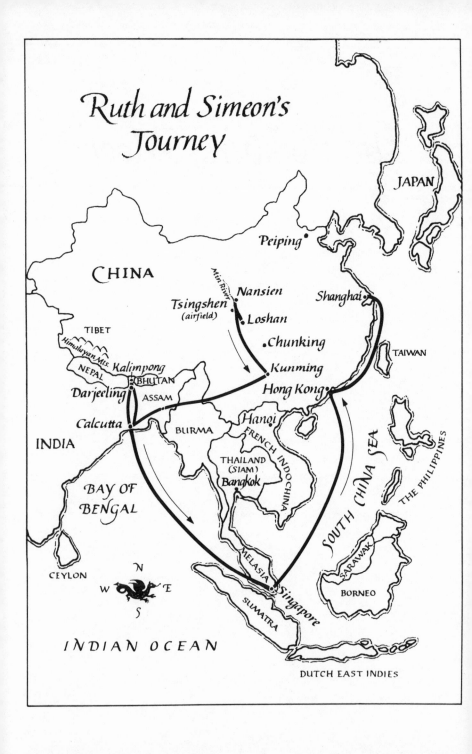

1

Our compound gate was huge, solid, and black. But in the bottom corner was a little door we usually came in or out by. One hot summer day in 1942 Simeon and I lolled on the verandah, bored to death, when the little door creaked. We looked up. It opened a crack, then wider, and the bottom of a cabbage inched through and hung there, halfway up the doorpost. The gatekeeper teetered back and forth on his toes, snickering. We pulled ourselves up and started slowly down the path.

Simeon frowned. "I wonder how it stays there."

"I bet I know," I answered suspiciously.

Suddenly the cabbage jumped into our compound. Underneath it was a black school jacket and pants with bare feet.

"Why're you wearing cabbage leaves?" I hollered.

Hongen lifted the cabbage-cap off his shiny shaven head and grinned. Then he threw it at me. I'm not good at catching and it landed at my feet. "They keep my head cool." But I could see they didn't; his head glistened with sweat. It was just another of his jokes. He was our amah's son and had thousands of ideas; sometimes they were good.

"Did you get pigeon kites for us?" I asked excitedly. "Shall we play kites?"

But he ignored my questions. "Today we jump," Hongen announced. "I will jump first. We will jump long. Over there." He pointed to the gardenia bushes. "And there. And there." His finger moved toward the compound wall and the tall plumy clump of bamboo. "Then we will jump from high, from the upstairs verandah." He jerked his chin up. "And then" —he looked slyly at me—"we will jump near the cow."

"No!" I argued, frightened by the jumping plans. "I want to play river bandits like the ones that took our American presents and sank the mail boat. This bench can be the boat and you can be the head bandit if you want."

"No! We will jump!" Hongen shouted.

He and I quarreled. Sometimes in English. Sometimes in Chinese. Sometimes in a hodgepodge of both.

"Oh no. Not again," Simeon muttered.

"You stink of milk, you milk-drinking Westerner!"

"You stink of garlic, you garlic-eating Chinese!"

"May you swallow a mouthful of uncooked rice and have it swell to one hundred!"

"Well, I hope you sail down the Min River in a

sampan the termites have feasted on for a hundred months!" I stuck out my tongue and waggled it at him.

"You are the one who has to sail down the Min River in the sampan. Not me! You will be the drowned one! Ha!" He pointed scornfully at me.

Poor Simeon stood with his hands on his hips. "Oh no," he said with a loud disgusted sigh, and wandered off to play with his little wooden truck under the mulberry tree, where he had started a road and an insect zoo. "I hope it's not like this at that school we have to go to.'

"You—" Hongen began again.

"Behave like proper children!" our amah commanded us. "You sound like those quarreling foxes out there." Hongen and I looked at each other, wondering what she was talking about. Then we grinned, pleased with the idea of a little excitement. Over the compound wall we could hear loud screeching and slapping from some angry women in our street. We dashed to the mulberry tree.

"Me first!"

"No! I!"

Hongen and I scrambled up the tree to look over the wall. By the time we got to the top, the shrieks of the dispute had died down, and people were just standing around, about half a dozen of them. But one woman, with a red hand-slap mark on her cheek, still skulked around the others as if she wasn't satisfied.

Our cow mooed unhappily. It was a mean old thing which kicked anyone who came near, except our cook, but even he had to tie the tail to the leg when he milked so it wouldn't hit his face. Our mother was always worrying about the cow; I guess because it had sharp horns and had broken loose a couple of times.

"We will play the game of guess," Hongen declared. This time I didn't argue and climbed down, below the level of the compound wall.

At the foot of the tree Simeon made squeaky noises for the pretend wheelbarrow he was pushing along the road he'd just dug with his pocketknife.

"I see a man. You guess," Hongen called down through the branches. "He is stopped. Hear him."

I listened. I could hear the *ting ting ting* of a dishmender tapping his little metal cleats into the two pieces of a broken bowl to fasten them back together. "Dishmender!" I shouted.

Again Hongen looked down Golden Horse Street. "Now is easy."

I listened to the *tramp tramp tramp* of several soldiers marching. "Soldier!" I yelled. "Do they have bayonets? I want to see their bayonets." I scrambled up to look. Two had bayonets slung over their shoulders. They all wore the usual patched uniforms.

The silly old cow went on with its bumbling and mooing. "That cow must have a tummyache," I commented.

"Then you will drink curdled milk tonight," Hongen answered, disgusted by the Western habit of drinking milk. In China it was for babies only.

I went back to my place. Suddenly I froze. I gripped the branches so hard my hands stung. "*Tss*,"

I hissed through my teeth at Hongen. He rubbed his hand over his shiny head and opened his mouth to ask me what in the world I meant. I shook my head frantically, then pointed with my chin to the side of the house. There stood the cow, a broken rope dangling from its neck. Slowly it grazed its way toward our tree and toward Simeon playing at the foot.

If I scream, I thought, it'll probably bolt and catch Simeon on those sharp gray horns, and he isn't big enough to climb the tree, and I don't think I could yank him up, not fast enough anyway.

I went on peering through the leaves, and saw the miserable cow graze its way nearer, very slowly, but always toward the mulberry tree. I could feel Hongen above me breathing hard. Then very slowly, so slowly I couldn't see but could only feel his weight shift, he slid his bare feet down the trunk, down, down toward the ground. I couldn't ask him what crazy scheme he had in mind. Our talking might startle the wretched beast.

Just as Hongen reached the second lowest branch, our mother came outside with a basket of cards she was cutting for Sunday school. Simeon went on making creaky sounds, as he carted bits of food for the insects in his zoo. Hongen and I were silent, but jabbing wildly through the air to point at the cow. Our mother put her hand to her mouth to call to us, but then she saw the cow. Her face went white as a gardenia; her brown eyes grew big as brass coins. Now she stood like an idol of fear. Very cautiously she set her basket on the grass. The hem of her blue gown fluttered in a tiny breeze.

The cow lifted its head, stared at our mother, and chewed and chewed in the slow, pondering way cows have, as if it had never had a mean thought. It started to amble toward her, flicking flies off with its tail as it came, but our mother scarcely noticed. Her eyes were almost out on stalks to reach Simeon.

The cow stopped at a patch of grass the coolie hadn't cut.

Suddenly, from the other side of the wall, the quarreling and slapping broke out again, very loud. "You child of a dog! You worthless flea!" There was a long scream. The startled cow raised its head and began lumbering toward the mulberry tree. Simeon looked up and turned to marble: deadly white and still. The cow lowered its head and charged straight at him. It caught his right arm with the tip of its horn, making a long red gash. But it hit its head against the tree trunk, mooed in pain, backed up, and lumbered off again toward its wooden water bucket.

Our mother snatched up Simeon; then she called back over her shoulder, "Stay there till I get the cook."

That night, just as usual, I sat on the edge of my bed near our father for the Bible reading. Opposite us, our mother sat holding Simeon in her lap, cradling his bandaged arm.

Our father read a story about a boy who left home and got lost. The only place he could find work to stay alive was on a farm with squabbly old pigs. They made him decide home wasn't such a bad place after all. When he read the stories our father always talked very earnestly, making it sound as if the whole Bible were written for us.

This time when he stopped talking, his face wore an expression I couldn't understand. He watched our mother rock a little back and forth, her cheek brushing against Simeon's hair. "Lillian, Lillian," he said in a regretful voice. "You spoil the boy. He's not a baby anymore. It'll just be harder when he's sent away to school next month."

She wiped her forehead with the handkerchief she always kept tucked in her watchband. "I know," she mumbled.

Simeon squeezed his head down, then kept absolutely still.

Our father stood up abruptly, holding his black leather Bible against him with his right hand and patting it with his left. "Nearly time for prayer meeting," he announced, and kissed the tops of our heads. "Good night, kiddies." We listened to his firm footsteps on the bouncy floorboards all the way to the front door.

Thunder rumbled. I moved to the other bed, close to our mother, careful not to joggle Simeon's arm. He glanced up, then tucked his face into her shoulder. Gently she pulled him back to look at the sky and chuckled softly. "It's nothing but a foolish old giant grinding stones in his stone mill for supper."

"Then what's the lightning?" he asked.

"He has to turn on his flashlight to see if he has enough." She patted my knee and gave me a look which said, "We're the big ones. We can take care of him." I smiled back at her.

The thunder passed. Our mother went to the prayer meeting and Simeon fell asleep in the bed beside mine. His arm, with the torn-sheet bandage on it, hung over the edge. It must have hurt because he kept twitching and touching it in his sleep. I looked at it for a while, then got up and laid it near his side.

The full moon rose over the city. I watched it until our amah came quietly down the long verandah and stood beside me against the railing, her busy hands resting for once. As she stared at the moon, her shoulders sagged and she gave a little moan. "It's bad—the bombers' moon," she said.

I looked up at her, puzzled. "The bombers' moon?"

"In the east all along the coast the Japanese make practice raids over the countryside, especially at full moon. It's practice, but they kill the farmers. The bombers' moon, the people call it."

"They're killing? With the full moon?"

She nodded. "Get into bed," she told me, and started tucking in the mosquito net.

I could imagine her out on the street, standing on the edge of the group of men and a few women, all with heads tilted back to see the newspaper pasted up on the wall near our post office. Someone who could read ran his finger down the lines of characters, calling out the words in a singsong voice for everyone to hear about the war.

"Is the war far away?"

"Right now it is far," she said heavily, and totter-walked back down the verandah on her little bound feet.

2

"Can't you help me?" I begged our amah, who was on the verandah ironing pillowcases. She looked sympathetic but shook her head. "For a little while?" She blew on the coals in the iron until they were glowing red. I remembered when Simeon had lost his pocketknife, she'd stopped her work even though the coals went out black. A boy was worth a hundred girls in China. I wished I were a boy.

I turned toward the bamboo grove, but Hongen stood smack in front of me rubbing his hand around and around his stomach. His face was sticky and grinning like a Buddha's. "I go on the street! I eat pork buns! I fly kites on the city wall with my friends!" that lucky old bean chanted.

I slipped past him.

"You do not know which thing I did on the street," he shouted indignantly. He dodged ahead of me and wrapped his arms around two thick bamboos so I couldn't get past.

I squeezed between the bamboos to his left and ran to the other side of the grove, peering into the dimness as I ran, trying to see if that was where I'd lost my doll.

"You do not ask questions. You do not know. What you think? Why you do not ask questions?" he shouted in frustration.

Finally Hongen stopped being a pest and helped me hunt for a while. Then he teased, "The poor mother has lost her daughter." He was so disgusted he went off to play with some Chinese friends on the street. For once I was glad to see him go.

I plonked on the verandah step and thought back to when I'd had the doll last. Back and back until I was remembering the time my doll came from Aunt Ruth, the big sister who raised our father after their mother died. I was special to her because I was named for her.

Two years before, she had sent me a rubber doll with blue eyes and curly brown hair pressed on its head. It arrived about a month after Christmas, at Chinese New Year's. It even wore a red knitted suit, which was the right celebration color.

I pretended that all the New Year's festivities in Nansien were welcoming my doll from America. Baskets, buckets, and doorways were decorated by pasting on squares of red good-luck paper, painted with golden characters. Gongs rang in the temples, firecrackers exploded all over the city, scary dragons paraded the streets, and extra candles burned before the idols in the houses. I celebrated by naming the doll Ruth.

Sometimes in bed at night, I'd sit it on my tummy, hold its hands, and think about America, where Aunt Ruth lived. "Everyone talks English!" I told her. "And they live in scrapers that touch the sky. And they go to—"

I was bumped out of my thoughts by Simeon. "Did you look under your chest of drawers?" he asked with a worried little frown, making him seem about a hundred years old.

"Of course, dummy," I answered. "You're too little to know good places."

"I'm big enough for a pocketknife," he said, holding it up. He shoved it back in his pocket, then asked, "What about the well? Did you look in the well?"

"The well?" I repeated, puzzled. "We're not allowed by the well. How could it get there?"

"Maybe Hongen threw it in. It'd float because it's rubber." He raised his eyebrows and looked hopefully into my face.

"That's a good idea, Simeon." He gave a pleased sigh.

We went behind the house to the well, which had a thick board cover we couldn't lift. For a few minutes we stood looking at it. "Come on, Simeon, let's try pushing it." We knelt and put our hands on the rough wood. "One, two, three. Push! One, two, three. Push!" Simeon grunted beside me, using his good hand. Finally we got it about halfway back and lay on our tummies with our heads hanging over the edge. I put my right hand on his back and looped my thumb through his belt.

We gasped at the two clear reflections staring up from the bottom of the well. "Maybe they're looking at us from America, where Aunt Ruth lives."

Simeon chuckled. "Mmm," he answered after a while. "What's a saycan?"

"It must be a sort of circus. I wonder why they go to circuses so early in the morning in America."

"It sounds exciting, with red rockets and balls bursting."

"And flags and banners waving."

"Like the dragon-boat festival," Simeon said longingly.

"They don't have balls bursting and rockets at the dragon-boat festival," I objected.

"No, but flags and banners."

"I wonder why they sing about circuses for their national anthem."

"I think God save our gracious is more sensible."

We dangled our heads over the edge and looked, enjoying the cool of the well on our hot faces.

Suddenly another reflection appeared at the bottom of the well, our father's. His two hands grabbed the clothes at our waists and dragged us back, pinching my right hand, which was still tucked in Simeon's belt. "Ruth!" He was so angry his voice shook. "Go to the study and wait there." Never had I heard him sound quite like that. My legs turned to molasses. I could hardly make them walk.

"It was my fault. I said to do it," Simeon squeaked.

"She's older." Our father gave an exasperated grunt. "She ought to know better." Out of the corner of my eye I saw him take Simeon by the hand to the verandah where our amah was still ironing.

I reached the study and sat down in the visitors' bamboo chair.

Our father's footsteps banged down the hall. His hands jerked me up and stood me in front of the large black desk. He sat himself in the chair facing me, mouth pinched shut, for what felt like a whole day.

"Ruth," our father said, "you are your brother's keeper." His iron voice chopped off the words. I shivered. Those words were from the story of Cain, who killed his brother Abel.

"I wasn't trying to kill him," I gasped. "We were looking for my doll."

The frown between his eyes grew deeper. His Adam's apple jerked up and down his throat several times before his preaching voice began. "That wasn't what I meant." His voice went on, explaining about "duties and responsibilities which increase as you grow older." Abruptly he leaned toward me. "You're leaving for school soon, Ruth. Your mother and I expect you to take care of Simeon, not lead him into dangerous places." He held my eyes with his stern gray ones. His voice shook. "Never, never go near the well. I have to spank you so you'll remember." He laid me across his hard, warm knees. I knew I deserved it.

That night I lay miserably in bed thinking about my doll. One mosquito droned inside the net. I slapped and missed, slapped again and missed. Then through the darkness came the *thud thud squeak* of our father walking along the verandah, and the lighter step of our mother. When they reached my bed they stopped. I watched through the mosquito net and listened to the faint murmur as they prayed for us, first our father, then our mother. Usually they'd go quietly on to Simeon's bed, but I must have been extra wriggly that night.

Our father asked, "Still awake, Ruthie?"

"Yes," I answered, trying not to cry. "I'm thinking about my doll." I pulled up the sheet and held a wad of it against my mouth.

"Tomorrow night we'll go to Wu Bao-Chuen's

shop for supper. You'll like that." He reached under the mosquito net and patted my shoulder. "Maybe we'll see if we can get you another doll."

"I don't *want* another doll," I cried out.

"Sssh," our mother cautioned. "Don't wake Simeon."

"I want *my* doll, the one Aunt Ruth gave me," I whispered fiercely. "The other dolls all look Chinese. I want my doll. It's the only one in Nansien that looks like me." I jammed the wad of sheet back over my mouth. Then an awful thought hit me: What if I have to leave for school without my doll?

3

All the next morning Simeon helped me with my search. But it was no good.

"Maybe," he suggested, "you could get a new doll when—"

"Dummy! I don't *want* a new doll. I want *my* doll that Aunt Ruth gave me."

"But if you can't find it—"

"Dummy! I've got to find it."

"But—"

"Dummy! Just help me look!"

"I'm sick and tired of you dummying me. You can jolly well find your own stupid doll!" He stomped off.

• • •

When we were ready to go to the food shop, our father said, "Ruth, wipe that look off your face and pull yourself together or you're staying home." I did not want to stay home. I loved Wu Bao-Chuen's food shop.

We went out. The street was crowded as a fair and almost as exciting. A man on a bike with shirttails flying zigzagged among the rickshaws, the coolies, and the people. He sheared past us and sideswiped a man with two baskets of cabbages hanging from a shoulderpole. One cabbage bounced right out on to the street. Simeon was nearly flattened in the sudden scramble of the crowd to grab it. He cringed and pulled his hurt arm protectively out of the way.

Along Five Brides Street, I got very hot and walked close to a watercarrier who was hurrying so fast the water slopped right over the rim of his thick wooden bucket. I let it splash onto my dress and shoes, which made me nice and cool, but squishy.

"What's your favorite thing?" I asked Simeon.

"Of what?"

"Of everything out here." I twisted back so I could watch his face as he walked along holding our mother's hand. His soft short hair stuck to his forehead in the heat. I grabbed our father and nearly jerked him over as I tripped against the foot of an opium addict lying at the side of the street.

"Better watch where you're going," our father said mildly, and took my hand.

"The bicycle shop," Simeon answered at last.

"The bicycle shop!" I turned back toward him. "You like that!"

"Mmm," he answered with a long, wistful sigh. "Just think if you could fix bikes all day. That's what I like the very best of all."

"Mr. Tan! Mrs. Tan!" A half-dozen children shouted our mother's and father's Chinese names and came running to hold hands. Two little girls skipped along beside us. A third girl caught up, carrying something in a blue cloth. I pulled our father forward, trying to see into the bundle. It was a Chinese doll.

A couple of kids touched my head. "See that hair!" All of them had straight black hair. Mine was curly and light brown. "See the noses! So high! So big!" I ducked a little sheepishly. We were the only Western children in Nansien.

"Foreign children, go to sleep. They have no quilt to cover them," a few more children chanted. Simeon and I grinned, trying to enjoy the nonsense but wishing we were less conspicuous.

"Have pity. Have pity," a voice whined from the side of the street. Bumping toward us was a beggar with no legs. He was strapped to a board on wheels, pushed by a little boy.

"Daddy, can't you give him something? Just this time?" The man looked so sad with his dirty hand held cupped to our father.

"It's no use, Ruthie. As soon as I put my hand in my pocket, there'll be a dozen more."

"But just this time, please."

"Someday you'll learn." He sighed and put his hand in his pocket for a few coins. Immediately from every alley and cluster of people other beggars appeared, whining and showing ugly injuries, some painted to look more gruesome. Hastily our father put the coins in the first man's hand, then pushed his way through the angry crowd of disappointed beggars, almost stepping on another opium addict.

All along the sides were little shops open right to the street. I sniffed as I walked along: leather, oilcloth, sandalwood; and because the children just had slits in their pants, and squatted on the street when they had to, there was that smell; then finally we got to the scrumptious fragrance of anise, garlic, soya sauce, and deep-fried pastries. Wu Bao-Chuen's! I was hungry as a tiger.

We stepped over the threshold and sat on benches on either side of a square table. Only two small tables stood on the earth floor of the little shop. Right away the crowd on the other side of the threshold began to comment, and kept it up the whole time we ate. A short man at the back kept jumping up for a better look.

"Can I have savory pork with bamboo shoots?" Simeon asked.

The short man popped up. "The little boy speaks well!" he said. Everyone laughed.

"Savory pork with bamboo shoots," Wu Bao-Chuen sang out to his cook up on a little platform at the back.

"Savory pork with bamboo shoots," the cook laughingly repeated, "for the little son of the house."

The short man popped up again. "The little boy has injured his arm," he said. The crowd pressed forward to get a better look.

I almost forgot about my doll, but not quite. Vaguely I wondered if Hongen had thrown it over the wall. I rested my chopsticks on the table as I thought.

The short man popped up. "The girl has dreams in her face," he joked. The crowd laughed and pointed.

When we had finished, our father told us, "We're going to visit the Ren family for a little while." We pushed our way through the crowd and down the street. Near the Rens' house a waxworker was modeling a figure.

"Can't we stay and watch while you go talk?" Simeon asked. Our mother looked doubtful; our father scratched the back of his head and frowned.

"Please, please," I begged, seeing there was a chance. "Look. He's making a little boy and see all the other kinds?" I pointed to the row of little wax figures on sticks—tigers, roosters, soldiers—all tucked into a rack at the side of his stand.

"Well," our father said slowly. "If you are *sure* to stay right here. And"—he put his hand on my shoulder—"take care of Simeon."

"We will. We will," we chanted, delighted not to have to sit and be polite while our father talked, probably Chinese Bible-talk.

On the waxworker's stand was an iron bowl with a little flickering flame underneath to warm the water in it. In the water were two lumps of wax softening, one orange and one black. The old man, who had a wooden leg and only a few hairs in his beard, took the wax in his hands, squeezed the lump, then pinched off bits in one place and pressed them on in another until he had a rough animal shape. Then he took a metal rod, rounded at one end, and stroked it over the figure, adding bits of black wax as he worked. Finally he scored the figure from top to bottom with short, quick strokes to give it a furry look. Taking two titchy brown glass beads, he pressed them into place. And there was another little tiger! By the time that clever old man was finished, Simeon's face was almost in the bowl.

"For the boy?" the old man said.

"I don't have any money." Simeon pulled his pockets inside out. Sadly the old man shook his head and slid the tiger into the rack beside one figure I hadn't noticed before: a fat baby with round instead of slanted eyes. That's funny, I thought, it's a bit like my doll.

"Come on, Simeon, let's see if there's anything else to watch."

"I don't want to watch anything else," he said in his Rock of Gibraltar voice. "I want to stay here."

"Come on," I teased, but Simeon didn't even answer. He pursed his lips and jerked his whole body back and forth in a NO NO NO motion he had.

I stood and scowled at the double cowlick on the crown of his head. The crowd tittered and pointed. I shot Simeon a scowl—his granite stubbornness wouldn't stop me—and started down the street. In the doorways women were nursing babies, sewing cloth shoes, sitting on little bamboo stools gossiping.

I stopped in front of one doorway. Something inside wasn't quite right. Two black scrolls on the wall facing me flanked a small wooden table where an idol sat. In front of the idol a candle flickered, erratically lighting up the face. As I looked, I suddenly grew furious! That idol wasn't made of plaster! That idol didn't have a broadly smiling Buddha face! That idol wasn't covered with glossy paint and bright colors! Instead, it had blue eyes and pressed brown curls and outstretched baby-doll arms and a naked rubber body.

"That's my doll!" I shouted.

The family all stopped what they were doing and stood threateningly in front of me. I stared up at them. Then I looked around at the watching crowd, suddenly turned silent. They pushed forward curiously. My eyes flicked back and forth. I could hardly breathe. What were they going to do, I wondered frantically. I locked my hands in front of me like a battering ram and struggled toward Simeon. The crowd didn't move. I put my head down and charged. Nobody said a word. I struggled, pushed, and shoved, half crazy with fear. I got to the edge of the crowd and ran. The crowd followed slowly behind.

Our father and mother were asking Simeon, "Which way did she go?" When they saw me they were about to scold, but I burst into such frightened, furious tears their mouths just stayed open.

"Where did you go? What happened?" they asked finally. Our mother took my hand and our father patted my shoulder, but I couldn't answer. Several children pushed me against our mother. Our father saw that still more people were gathering to see what all the fuss was about.

"Come," he said, and took us into the Rens' house.

It was several minutes before he could make any sense of what I was saying. Finally he turned to Mr. Ren, a small man with a gold front tooth which glittered as he talked. "Do you know this family?"

Mr. Ren looked troubled. "Yes," he answered slowly, and stared past our father's right arm. "I may be able to get it for you."

"But I want it now!" I cried out. "I know it's my doll!"

"Ruth!"

I shrank back next to our mother and Simeon.

The two men talked quietly for several minutes, nodding a little and frowning. Finally they clasped their own hands and bowed to each other. We left.

It was dusk. Families had begun to light their little flickering oil lamps and to set them near their doorways all down the street. Only a few people followed us; most had gone home to eat rice.

Suddenly I chuckled and glanced up, but our father's face was stern, not ready for funny thoughts. Simeon rode on his shoulders, his bandaged arm resting on our father's head. I reached up and tapped his shoe. "What do you think Aunt Ruth will say when she hears about people worshipping my doll?" I asked him and giggled.

"Huh?"

"Aunt Ruth thought she sent me a baby-doll, but really she sent me a baby-idol." We walked on. Suddenly I asked, "They will give it back, won't they, Daddy?" But he didn't answer.

After breakfast a week later, the gatekeeper brought in my poor, filthy doll, naked and speckled with smeary black from the incense. He held it out by the foot, then left without a word of explanation to our mother. She knew better than to ask.

"We'll clean it," our mother said. "Then I'll sew

a frock for it." I looked up to see if she meant it. I'd never seen her sew anything. By afternoon she'd finished. Simeon and I watched her put in the last knot and slide the dark blue frock over the head. She put the doll into my hands, then combed her fingers through Simeon's soft, newly cut hair. "Now all three of you are ready for school," she said.

4

In front of the dining-room window, with its brass corners and latches glinting in the sunlight, stood the knobby blue steamer trunk. Our father and the cook had carried it down from the luggage room three days ago. On top of it were folded two patchwork quilts: nine-inch squares of gingham alternating with nine-inch squares of embroidered Bible verses.

Simeon ran the tip of his finger over the green embroidery threads. "What's this one say?"

" 'There was nothing in the ark save the two tables of stone. I Kings 8:9. Norah Evans,' " our mother read.

"That's a funny verse to choose."

"Perhaps Norah Evans wanted you to know how important the Ten Commandments are. That's what was on the tables of stone."

"It must have been a huge box for two stone tables."

"That just means flat stones. About like this maybe." She measured off the size with her hands.

"Would it still make it heavy?" Simeon asked.

"Probably."

He looked oddly pleased. Then he said hurriedly, as if to distract our mother, "It must have taken those St. Bridget's Church ladies a terribly long time to sew all those."

"They meet once a week to sew for missionaries. They sent them when you were born," our mother said. "Your granny used to go when she could see well enough. I've been keeping them for when you went away to school." She put down the wretched needle, which stuck at almost every stitch, and pushed back her hair. "That's enough for now. Come, little sister," she said to our amah. "We'll have some tea."

The daytime was too hot to sew the pesky little school laundry numbers onto the dresses, trousers, and other clothes, which lay in counted piles on a trestle table set near the trunk. At night, when it was cooler, the flickering oil lamp wasn't really quite bright enough for sewing.

"But we'll get it done in time," our mother said, as if challenging that sticky needle to a contest.

Late that night I woke up from a scary dream. I dreamed our family was turned into straw people by the Japanese. A harsh, biting wind blew out of the bombers' moon and blew and blew until we were all blown to wisps. I pulled out the mosquito net, slid out of bed, got my doll by the arm, and tiptoed over to Simeon's bed. His face was smiling a little. In a

— *25* —

few days it'll be just us two, I thought. Carefully, I untucked his net and slid in beside him, something I hadn't done for a long time.

Seven days later the dining room looked a mess. Two pairs of socks and a sweater which just wouldn't fit in the trunk had been tossed aside on a chair. An ironed dress, shirt, and pants hung in front of one window. Our two suitcases, half filled, lay open on the floor. Several pages of instructions from the school had slid to the floor and scattered. The furniture was higgledy-piggledy.

"Simeon, do stay still," our mother said in frustration, when his pant-leg hem kept turning out first too short, then too long. She reached for the spool of white thread which was tangled with the measuring tape. Her face was crimson and her hair curled like the Wild Woman of Borneo, as she sometimes called herself. She knelt in front of the chair Simeon was standing on.

"Will my suitcase be heavy?" he asked.

"Oh, I don't know. Probably. Do stay still."

"The thimble dropped again," I pointed out unhelpfully.

"Get it, Ruth! Use your head a little bit!"

"What must be done will be done," our amah said comfortably, though even she looked more scattered than usual. She had pins and threaded needles stuck in here and there down the front of her gown, and her face, peppered with smallpox scars, was a bit flushed.

"Ruth, Simeon, come and meet Miss Lin," our

father said in a too jolly voice from the doorway. Beside him stood a woman who didn't even reach his shoulder. She was neat as a needle.

"I can't. Mummy's sewing me," Simeon happily called from his chair. In the last few days he'd seemed cheerfully excited about our new school.

Our father gave an uncomfortable cough. "Ruth, this is Miss Lin." She smoothed an invisible wrinkle in her gown. "She is a fine, responsible Bible-woman who will escort you to your school. She has some teaching to do in Loshan, then she'll bring you back for Christmas."

"I take you on boat. I take luggage to school. I take care tickets. I take care you . . ." she went on and on in her fussy voice, occasionally chucking me under the chin as if I were a baby. I bowed, glad to be able to look down. I did not like Miss Lin. She was too neat and too talkative. I wished our amah could take us to our emergency school, but she wasn't any good at making arrangements and traveling around. Miss Lin was. Our father led her to his study.

Simeon and I grimaced. "She's not helping me with *my* luggage," he said. "I'm big enough to carry my own."

Our mother went on adjusting the pant-leg hem.

Our amah gave one of her rare chuckles. "Your Miss Lin. She talks."

Getting us to school was a complicated business. There had to be enough rain in the Min River, and no river bandits or cholera epidemics. Besides all that, the Japanese soldiers had captured our regular school and put all four hundred kids in a concentration camp someplace in North China. A new little school was starting in Loshan. This was why I'd been kept at home a little longer than usual, so Simeon and I could go together.

At noon a couple of days later, two coolies came to our house, picked up our steamer trunk by its two leather handles, and loaded it on their baggage cart. I carried my suitcase, a brown one with a rope handle, and Simeon carried his, a green one with brass corners.

"Do you want me to carry your case?" our mother asked Simeon. She wore a pretty flowery dress instead of her usual blue gown, and she had brushed her hair until it lay softly curled around her face. Her big brown eyes kept smiling at us. "Do you want me to carry it?"

"Oh no," Simeon answered far more happily than I expected for the morning of going away. "I'm a big schoolboy now. I can carry it easy." He made a great show of lugging the heavy thing down to the gate. "This is a very important suitcase, isn't it?" he asked as he let it bang against his right knee.

"Yes, dear. It has everything you'll need on the boat, so take good care of it."

"Oh, I am. I really am," Simeon assured her, frowning importantly.

At the gate, we said goodbye to Hongen and our amah. Simeon hugged her around her middle, then I did. "See you at Christmas," I said, looking up into her face.

"That is my good hope." She patted us.

"If the termites haven't feasted on your sampan so you drown," Hongen added cheerfully.

Simeon and I rode in the first rickshaw, our suitcases at our feet. Our mother rode in the second, Miss Lin in the third, and the luggage cart bumped along behind. Our father, on his black bike, rode sometimes on one side, sometimes on the other, keeping us all together. As usual there was a crowd of kids shouting and running alongside, dodging to keep clear of the bike.

At the river a troop of soldiers plowed through the crowd toward a large raft tied near the shore. We tried to use the path they made, but water carriers and coolies shouldering loads filled it first. In the river, fleets of sampans rocked on the water, jostling one another.

Simeon and I stayed close to our mother while Miss Lin and our father went to see where among all those heaving boats our sampan was tied.

"You can put your cases down while we wait," our mother said. But Simeon clutched his as if his life depended on it.

Suddenly he let go of the handle, straddled the case with his short legs, and started searching in his shirt pockets, his pants pockets, and on the ground. "My knife, where's my pocketknife?" he asked, very worried.

"Oh, Simeon, don't be a dope," I told him. "It's probably in your suitcase." The pesky thing was lost again. It's a wonder it didn't stay lost.

"Here it is," he said, smiling with relief as he fished it out of the bottom of his pocket. He fiddled with it while our mother craned over the crowd to see if our father was coming soon. Just as he and Miss Lin reached us, Simeon cried out, "I've cut myself, and look my shirt's all messy with blood." He held up his cut thumb and showed the smeary place on his sleeve and down the front of his shirt. It looked like an awfully big mess for such a little cut.

"We'll just have to get out one of your clean shirts," our mother said, stooping to unfasten his suitcase. She pulled back the little brass catch, opened the case, and stared. Slowly she turned to look up at Simeon, who was smiling like a prince at a victory. There was nothing in the case except two largish flat stones.

"Now I'll miss the boat. Now I won't have to go to school. Will I?" Simeon said. There was silence.

Then Miss Lin craned forward from the waist and raised her steel-rimmed glasses a little. "Oh! Oh!" she crowed. "Oh! Oh!"

There was another silence.

"Will I?" Simeon said, his smile beginning to fade. "I will miss the boat, won't I?"

Suddenly our father laughed harder than he had for a very long time. "Oh, sonny, sonny, that was pretty clever, pretty pretty clever." He dumped out the two stones and picked up the suitcase and Simeon. "You and I are going to have to move like greased lightning." He called back over his shoulder, "Stay here. Tell the boatman."

"I tell boatman." Miss Lin hustled off.

I looked at our mother. Her face was rosy, her eyes shining with laughter. "So that's why he was so interested in the tables of stone," she chuckled. "I did wonder."

They were back in short order. Simeon slid off the bicycle bar and swaggered beside our father, carrying his green suitcase. "I'm the only man of the family going downriver," he informed me.

"Man of the family!"

"Yep!"

We bowed our heads. Our father thanked God for Simeon and me and prayed for a safe journey. The hugs, kisses, laughing, and crying were over in no time. "See you at Christmas. See you at Christmas," we called to each other as Miss Lin got the two of us to the river's edge.

We picked our careful way over the string of tippety sampans until we reached the right one. Miss Lin sat down with Simeon on one side and me on the other. The boatman took his long bamboo pole with the iron tip, and pushed out to the middle of the river.

Our father stood on the shore with his arm around our mother, something I'd never seen him do in public, because in China it was not proper. She waved her brave little white handkerchief. As the boatman poled us into the river, our mother was swallowed by the busy crowd. Our father was so tall we saw him until a pagoda got in the way.

But the river was exciting. A sampan sits so low in the water you feel more as though you're in the river than on the river. Water swished and swirled all around us as the bank sailed slowly by.

"Look at those ducks, Simeon." I pointed. "They've got their own little bridge onto their boat."

"Where? Where?" He squinted at the farms along the bank, then chuckled. "Two fell off." Soon he began humming the grunty song of a gang of work-men heaving something big along the bank.

For several days we watched, listened to Miss Lin's boring chatter, ate rice, slept, moped, did our teeth, and spat into the river.

Toward the end of the fourth day the boatman was very busy navigating our way through the swift currents near Loshan. The high red cliffs on either side of the Min River funneled us right to where we were going.

"Look! Ruth, look!" Simeon shouted, suddenly distracted from his moping. He pointed along the cliff. "No, Ruth, this side. Look!"

I craned around. "Oh my goodness!" I gasped, and squinted up through the haze. So high above us we had to tilt our heads back as far as they would go was the giant Buddha carved right into the red rock cliff. He had such a huge face, trees and bushes grew on the ledges of his eyebrows, on the top of his head, and in his ears. Our family, our amah, and Hongen could have sat on one toenail. The rock under his foot had watermarks from the rising and falling of the river.

I wished Miss Lin would shut up, but she was fussily asking if we'd remembered to put this, that, and the other into our suitcases.

Then, before we knew it, the river was behind us. We were standing in front of the high, solid, black wooden gate in the wall around the compound of our new school. Our hearts banged in our chests. Miss Lin banged the gate.

5

There were no children anywhere! Simeon tossed me an accusing glance. I looked away at the three high wooden swings and two empty seesaws, surrounded by a lot of trampled grass. Then I stared straight ahead at a big rambling building with gray tiles, whitewashed walls, and verandahs at either end. But no children stared back.

The gatekeeper grunted and pointed to a brown door in the middle of the building. The outlines were already beginning to blur in the dull afternoon light. "Come. Come. Come," Miss Lin said to Simeon and me, as if she were repeating the first page of her English primer. "Come now with me." She picked up her black suitcase with her name pasted on it, so we picked up ours to follow her single-file down the dirt walkway.

Miss Lin rapped on the door. Simeon and I stood waiting together a little behind her. Soldier footsteps clicked inside. The knob turned with a jerk and the door flew open. A long pole of a woman looked down at us. She was gray from bottom to top: stockings, dress, hair. Right at the top was a pewter pendant with a complicated monogram on it. Even her face was grayish, because the light was dim. "This way, please," she snapped, and turned down a dark hall that seemed to go on forever. Even Miss Lin was struck dumb.

The pole-woman stopped at a long, unpainted stairway. "Leave your suitcases there." She pointed to a spot below the square newel post.

Suddenly I realized I was hearing a murmur. Maybe it was children.

"Simeon, come," the woman ordered. He looked helplessly at me, then followed her through a door with a white painted word on it. The door closed. I waited, wishing we could have gone together. In a few minutes the woman came out and motioned Miss Lin and me into the other bathroom, where a long row of white enamel washbasins sat on two wooden slats, stretching all the way down the room. A towel hung by each basin. Just inside the door was a huge clay water pot, big enough to hold both Simeon and me.

"Go to the end, Ruth. You'll find a basin with your laundry number on it. Bring it here." She dipped water from the pot into the basin. I was very glad I didn't have bound feet, it was so hard to keep the water from slipping and slopping over the blue rim. Miss Lin and I washed.

The woman led us through another door into a lamplit room filled with children, thirty or forty of them. I'd never seen a crowd of Western children before. They all seemed about the same size as Simeon and me, though it was a little hard to tell in the lamplight.

Eagerly I looked along the rows sitting at the four long tables that stretched down the whole room. One girl had curly red hair. I'd never even heard of such a color for hair. I tripped on a floorboard and went flat on my face. Miss Lin talked. Several children snickered. "And in front of Miss Elson!" they whispered.

"Miss Lin, come with me. Get up, Ruth. Watch where you're going," Miss Elson said.

I scrambled to my feet, too mortified to look anywhere but at the space on the bench. I didn't even try to eat whatever was on the plate in front of me. My first day at school and I had to do a dumb thing like that.

Suddenly I felt a warm hand slide into my lap. I put both mine around that hand and slowly looked up into the laughing blue eyes of Anne, the girl with red hair. She pressed her other hand over her mouth to stifle her giggles. I copied her.

"What's *this* stuff?" Simeon asked from beside me. He held up his enamel mug.

"*Do jang*," Anne said comfortably, "soybean milk. There aren't any school cows. That's what we drink."

"All the time?" he gasped. Anne nodded. Simeon's mouth set. "Boy, I can't wait till Christmas, when we go home."

Anne looked at me. "Is he yours?"

"Mine? My what?"

"Is he your brother, or did you just come together?"

"He's mine."

"Lucky."

The brass bell rang. Everyone shot into line. Simeon and I sat staring. "Come! Quick!" Anne hissed.

Miss Lin disappeared with Miss Elson and that was the last we saw of her.

"Don't you want to play with your truck?" I asked Simeon one afternoon and pointed to the boys under the pomegranate tree.

"No."

"Well, what do you want to do?"

He shrugged.

Averell and Norman joined us. "You want to know what he does?" they asked. "He cries at night. In his bed." Simeon turned away, not even bothering to defend himself. "Mrs. MacGuire tucks him in and he stops, but he starts again when she takes her lamp out." The two boys looked at me as if expecting me to do something.

I remembered one afternoon at home in the week before we left. Our mother and I were sitting together. "I'm worried about Simeon at school. He hasn't your bounce," our mother said, as though I were a grown-up friend.

"I'll take care of him," I promised her. "I'll talk to him and play games with him."

"You're not just a pretty face." She took my face in her hands and smiled, sadly though.

"Am I pretty?" I asked, pleased.

Our mother chuckled. "Yes, snookie, pretty enough, but that's an expression my Irish aunt used when she wanted to say somebody could think or act as well as be a decoration in life." I sat as tall as I could.

"Simeon," I said, and took a deep breath, "you're not allowed to cry. You're at school now." He looked down at the toes of his shiny brown shoes, kept shiny by a lot of worried brushing and careful walking, but he didn't answer.

Over the next few days I tried to do nice things to comfort him, like saving one of my Sunday candies for him. I tried to tell him our mother's stories, but that was pretty dumb because I wasn't our mother and I couldn't remember the right words, and besides, it didn't do any good.

Maybe I should help him be tough, I thought a couple of weeks later, especially for inspection, since that scares the living daylights out of him. "Watch me, Simeon." I took his head in both my hands. "Watch my jaws. That's right. Clamp your teeth as tight as you can."

"I am."

"Well, do that at inspection. It stops you crying."

"I'll try."

"Good. And don't look at Miss Elson. Look at the wall or her skinny neck, or anything, but not her face."

"I'll try."

Next morning, right after breakfast we filed into the large bare common room and lined up as usual for inspection in front of Miss Elson's grim glare. Her eyes traveled slowly over the first boy, inspecting for an untidy collar, a torn sleeve, missing buttons, a lost hanky.

"Next!" Miss Elson barked. Simeon stepped in front of her, teeth clamped so tight his cheeks bulged. "Simeon, show me the bottom of your shoes." Slowly he lifted his feet, one after the other, to show the soles of his shoes.

"Next!" Paul moved up.

Since that worked, I decided to try to toughen him some more after classes. Anne could help me this time. "Remember that story we had in Scripture class this morning?" I asked her. "The one where God calls the scaredy-cat Gideon a 'mighty man of valor'? Let's have a ceremony and call Simeon that. Maybe it'd make him brave, too."

"Not likely," she answered. "Simeon wouldn't even know what a 'mighty man of valor' is."

"But we could call him other brave things."

She shrugged. "May as well try." Simeon stood forlornly by, not even listening to our schemes.

The spiraling shriek of a siren rose from the swings, where several kids were playing air raids.

In order to make our ceremony special and important, we led Simeon under the feathery branches of the maidenhair tree. "This is the Tree of the Strength of the Lord," we told him.

Anne took one of his limp hands in both of hers; I took the other in both of mine. "Now you are a brave boy," Anne said in her grown-up voice.

Simeon looked puzzled and jerked his chin toward me. "But she told me I'm a cowardy custard."

"Not anymore." Anne lifted his hand high toward the branches of the tree. Several stitches in the underarm seam of her blouse popped.

I raised his other hand. "You're lionhearted."

"You're ad . . . ad . . . What's that word?"

Three kids tore by, yelling, arms outstretched as Japanese bombers.

"Adventurous?"

"You're adventurous."

Simeon looked more and more confused and began to cry. "You're just teasing me." He shuffled off dejectedly to the pomegranate tree and sat in the loose dirt.

"Hey! That's where we're bombing next," a couple of boys shouted. "Move!" Simeon shifted to the other side of the tree.

"Simeon," I said, "give me your pocketknife and I'll dig you a road."

"No."

"Why not? What's the matter with you, anyway?" I asked crossly.

"You'll lose it."

"Me! You're the one that loses it."

"I always find it again." He turned and scrubbed away the tears, leaving dirty streaks, because his hands had been muddling in the dirt as he sat leaning against the tree.

"And *you* could be Mole," a voice said. Paul sat down by Simeon, holding his green-covered book as usual. He wore a light brown sweater, damp at the cuffs, where he absently chewed when he looked at his book. He went on, "When you're Mole you'll have such fun coming with me on the river. Wouldn't you like that?"

Slowly Simeon turned toward Paul and frowned. "Whatever are you talking about?"

Paul's dreamy blue eyes shone. "This," he said, holding up his book. It was one of the few books at school. The Japanese bombing all down the coast prevented any texts arriving from England, so the teachers wrote all our lessons on the blackboard. We knew Paul's book was special. "This," he said again, and opened to the title page. "I'm Ratty and you can be Mole. Wouldn't you like to be Mole? It's all in *Wind in the Willows*."

Simeon thought for a while. "I suppose," he said, very doubtfully. "Are there machines in it?"

"Oh yes," Paul answered. "There are motorcars and some get smashed up, and trains for escaping, and boats and gypsy wagons." Simeon sat away from the pomegranate tree and leaned a little toward Paul. "Do you want to see?" Paul pushed his pale gold hair out of his eyes and opened the book.

"I guess," Simeon said. Paul showed him picture after picture. Most of them were little line drawings, and a few large watercolor illustrations that made you long to be in a place so beautiful and magical.

"Boom! Boom! Boom!" the Japanese bombers growled, making us all jump. They dropped handfuls of pebbles on their patch under the tree. "You guys'll get hit if you don't watch out." We didn't move.

On their next attack they came a little closer. Paul went on slowly turning pages, but the rest of us eyed the bombers, sort of daring them to hit us. They stopped and gave us dirty looks, glanced at each other, then trickled their pebbles onto the toes of our shoes.

"You dopes!" I hollered. "Why—"

The bell rang for supper.

"All clear!" Anne sang out. I laughed; so did one of the bombers.

6

"Anne," I gasped, dashing up and grabbing her hand. "I nearly had to walk with Monica. That dope. She said she wouldn't walk with you because you're a fatty." Anne grimaced. Monica often taunted her. I glanced back down the crocodile to where that dope stood by herself. She'd have to hold a teacher's hand, which she'd rather do anyway. "Where'd Mr. Kingsley say we're going this Sunday?"

"The chrysanthemum gardens," one of the boys told us. "It's the best place for playing air raids and bombers."

I turned around. "You've got air raids on the brain."

"Just wait," he said ominously.

"What a dope!"

"No, he's not." Anne's voice was more somber than usual.

The gatekeeper opened the door and lifted the smaller children over the high threshold. Mr. Kingsley led the way down the street for our Sunday walk; Mrs. MacGuire brought up the rear with Monica.

"Big nose! Big nose!" the Chinese children yelled enthusiastically. They trotted along beside us, pointing at our spectacular noses. Half a dozen small Chinese boys stopped in a group, pressed each other's little flat noses, then were so convulsed with laughter they had to sprint to catch up again.

The crocodile made its way through the usual crowds, down the winding street to the edge of the city. By the time we reached the gardens, only four persistent tag-alongs were with us. "Big nose!" they yelled once more for good measure, and sauntered off.

The garden was enclosed on three sides by a high tiled wall; the fourth side was open to rice fields as far as you could see. There were twenty or thirty plots of flowers, each with a different color of chrysanthemum: white, bronze, pink, yellow.

An old, hunchbacked man shuffled from one plot to the next, snipping off dead flowers. Often he stopped and let the ends of his thin fingers run down a stem, knocking off dead leaves, touching the plants as if they were his pets. He didn't even glance at us, or notice the boys making their airplane swoops around the walls.

Simeon put out his hand to stroke a soft yellow flower. Immediately the old man hustled over, scolding and muttering. Simeon stepped back and stared crossly out toward the rice fields.

Suddenly he tensed, leaned forward, and nudged Paul. "You see that?"

"See what?"

"Over there. No. Look."

"That pile of junk?"

"It's not junk," Simeon said impatiently. "Mr. Kingsley, can we go see it?"

"What is it, Simeon?"

"Look. Please, may we?" Simeon held his breath,

then started anxiously biting his nails, while Mr. Kingsley rubbed his thumb up and down his beaky nose and pondered in the most maddeningly slow way.

"We'll have to stay together and walk carefully." He led us across the narrow little dike between two rice fields, onto a large dry patch of ground where the crashed airplane was heaped.

The cockpit and one wing, which stuck straight up, were burned; the rest lay in twisted pieces. For some reason it hadn't been picked over and the bits hauled home to repair buckets or hoes or cart wheels. Simeon ran from part to part, not touching, but examining it as though he had it in mind to fix it. Finally he hunkered down by the tailpiece. "Come here, Paul. Look at this." He pulled out his pocket-knife, opened the screwdriver blade as if he could put it to use, and explained to Paul what he wished he could do. Paul frowned, trying to understand.

The rest of the boys walked about looking, pointing, nattering, occasionally asking Malcolm's opinion. Malcolm was the oldest boy in our school and the obvious authority on anything.

Anne and I stood in a huddle with the girls. "Boys are stupid," she said matter-of-factly. "What's there to like about that thing?"

On the way back to school Simeon told me, "Two good things have happened to me. I've seen a real crashed airplane."

"What's the other one?"

"I'm Paul's friend. I'm Mole."

"He's nice," I answered, "but isn't he, well, kind of funny?"

Simeon looked at me indignantly. "Ruth," he said, solemn as our father, "Paul's my friend! He's my *own* friend."

A few days later we were sitting in the dining room, eating bean soup and swinging our legs, when suddenly a siren wailed faintly above our chatter.

"What's that?"

"Air-raid siren," Anne said. "Look out the window behind you." I turned and squinted. "See that tall pole with a huge red cloth ball on top?" I nodded. "That's the first warning."

"There's another one jerking up."

"Second warning. Japanese planes must be pretty near now. Dinner in the dugout again," she said, trying not to be scared.

Miss Elson stood up. "Everyone carry his bowl into line without spilling," she barked.

Malcolm headed the line as usual, not even glancing at her. He always moved like the wind but didn't knock things over, and for some reason he seldom made Miss Elson cross.

The siren wailed eerily on and on, filling our ears, the dining room, the school compound, the whole city. Simeon was so scared his hands shook enough to make his soup jiggle. But I thought it might be interesting to eat in a dark dugout where we were never allowed to play. We filed out singing, "Onward, Christian Soldiers."

The dugout was a shallow cave further hollowed out, entered by a doorway made of thick pieces of wood covered with lots of dirt. It had a musty, damp-earth smell. We sat on the rough wooden benches, ate our soup, then waited. Mr. Kingsley leaned forward in the half-darkness and prayed, asking the Lord Almighty to "grant us protection from death and destruction." Somebody began to scratch. My foot itched. Waiting makes you very itchy. A drop fell from the damp earth roof. Miss Elson's nose whistled.

And then we heard it: a miserable hum, as though all the trucks in the Japanese Army were starting their engines on a distant field. But instead of trucks it was airplanes roaring toward our little dugout with throttles wide open, coming at us from every direction. The ground shook.

The roaring passed over and shrank away. We heard the *crash tinkle tinkle* of glass smashing and dropping on cement. We thought we heard explosions in the distance. I felt Simeon turn stiff against my arm. I put my soup bowl in my lap and held my hands over his ears, as I could barely see Mrs. MacGuire doing for Monica, who was so scared she whimpered. Malcolm also had his hands over his little brother Norman's ears.

A big stillness settled into the dugout, but still we waited and held our empty soup bowls.

Suddenly we heard it again, the roaring which got louder and louder until it made the ground shake and made bits of dirt from the dugout roof sprinkle into our hair. Then it shrank away. There was more smashing glass and distant explosions. Simeon was shivering when we came out.

One afternoon, the air raid came on so fast we ended up in a scramble of children, servants, and teachers, all trying to push into the dugout at once. The wish to actually see those dreadful planes gripped me so hard I forgot any good sense. Somehow I managed to vanish from the others and make my way to the verandah farthest from the dugout. I was the last person in the world; there wasn't even a servant pegging out laundry. The drone had begun and was growing louder. I stood with my head tilted to the sky, my hands plastered over my ears. Suddenly I saw them, and watched with fascinated horror as fifteen or sixteen dots in perfect formation grew into planes.

I was snatched up. "You naughty girl! You naughty, naughty girl!" a furious voice hissed. Mr. Kingsley ran into the dugout just as the planes flew overhead. He forgot to put me down. His arms felt tight with anger.

As soon as the All Clear sounded, Mr. Kingsley gripped my wrist and marched me back to the spot where I'd been standing. He didn't have to say anything, but he asked, "Where would you be now if I hadn't found you?" He took my chin, turned my face up to his, and looked at me, his eyes burning. Shrapnel lay all around: pieces of broken glass, chunks of cement. He marched me to Miss Elson to be spanked.

I went outside, back near the verandah where the other kids were bending over, picking up pieces of shrapnel for their collections.

"What if you'd got killed?" Simeon asked as he sidled up to me and showed me his prize piece. Tears rolled down his face.

"Well, I didn't."

His tears came faster. "I want to go home to Daddy and Mummy for Christmas."

"Silly, you can't. There's a war on," I snapped, turning my back to him. "Anyhow, what would happen to Paul if you went home?"

Simeon stopped crying and thought for a while. "No," he said slowly, "I guess I can't go home. I have to stay with my friend."

"Malcolm said he heard one of the teachers talking about maybe the whole school will have to leave here," I said to Anne.

"But it's nearly Christmas! Anyhow, where'd we go? Tibet's about all that's left. My dad's making maps about Tibet. We have maps all over our house at home. Not like these dumb empty walls."

"Why?"

"Just because he likes maps. Did Malcolm say when?"

"He said he couldn't hear properly, but that's what he thought they said. What do you want to do?"

Every lull in the chatter in the common room was filled by the knocking of the rain on the windows on that rotten December afternoon. The only good thing about it was that rain and thick clouds stopped the air raids.

The common room was sparsely furnished. A grass mat covered the floor; sometimes, when we weren't paying attention, our toes would catch in a loose strand and send us flying. The walls were whitewashed and felt sandy-rough if you ran the tips of your fingers over them. There were no pictures. The windows had no curtains, but the windowpanes made up for that with the bubbles and flaws in the glass. When you looked through those bubbles and flaws, tipping your head back and forth, the trees and swings outside looked really cockeyed. At one end of the room there was a shelf stacked with the games some of the kids had brought from home: snakes-and-ladders, checkers, ludo, Parcheesi. But that day not many of us felt like playing games. Most of the kids sat around in clusters doing nothing in particular.

Anne and I lolled near a window. Simeon and Paul hunched nearby, and as usual Paul held his book. "You know what I feel like?" he asked. Simeon chewed on the end of his pocketknife and slowly shook his head. "Well, I feel like Mole when he wasn't home for Christmas. 'He subsided forlornly on a tree stump' and 'He had a sob which refused to be beaten' and that's what I feel like."

"How come you know what it says?" Simeon asked irritably. "You can't read that much yet, and anyhow, your book's not open."

"That's my favorite chapter, but that's not all the words. Mummy read it to me lots of times." Then Paul told about Christmas at home. He was much younger than his five brothers and sisters. They were at the regular school, which was now in Weihsien concentration camp in the north of China. On Christmas Day, while his father was at Chinese church, his mother read to him. At night they ate a big Christmas dinner with a plum cake his mother and their cook had made weeks before.

Anne and I slid along the windowsill toward the boys. Overhead, a floorboard creaked. Probably a servant putting away laundry.

"What about you?" Paul asked.

"Mummy helps us decorate a little tree," Simeon said, and told about our box of tiny pewter ornaments, which our mother had brought from her home in England. There were two boots, a sprig of holly, a train engine, and lots of others, but all different. "And we eat a roast chicken for Daddy because he always eats turkeys in America. And Daddy puts on his red bathrobe, and ties on a new mop-beard, and carries a pillowcase with cookies and tangerines and presents. He's Santa Claus."

"He really does that?"

Simeon nodded slowly and stared out at the rain with a half-smile on his face.

A servant brought in four oil lamps and set them on their holders.

"We . . . we . . ." Anne started, but her giggles choked her.

Several idlers wandered over. "What's going on?"

". . . have a picnic," Anne finally said.

"You're having a picnic!"

"I think we're talking about Christmas," I explained.

"That's what we do, a big picnic . . ." We all laughed, wondering what she was going to tell us next. You never knew with Anne's family. "On the floor for Christmas." She gestured, indicating a perfect mountain of food on the floor. "My mum and dad are New Zealanders. At Christmas it's summer!"

she went on. "They used to go to the beach for a picnic and a swim on Christmas afternoon. It's an exciting place with hot springs that make the mud go plop, plop, plop."

"Well, I'll be!"

Anne nodded. "After presents Dad tells about rascally things he did when he was a kid. And about his exploring." He took three or four weeks every year, and went with a guide to the borders of Tibet, where he was making maps. Her mother had a funny Maori word for him, which meant someone with a restless spirit.

Paul sighed as though such a Christmas really appealed to him. But Simeon just shook his head.

A week later it was school Christmas. We had church services and a special dinner which ended with pink sugar mice. Mr. Kingsley dressed up as Father Christmas and gave us each a present. I got a tea set for my doll; Simeon, a toy airplane with a rubber band to make it go; and Anne, a family of wooden dolls which fit one inside the other.

Paul's was the most magical present I've ever seen. "You want a turn?" he asked me as Simeon's plane glided by. I took Paul's glass paperweight carefully in both hands and stared into it. Inside the thick glass globe was a little boy with a scarlet hat, a blue coat, and a yellow scarf. I shook it. Suddenly the little boy was in the middle of a whirling snowstorm.

In the afternoon we played games, but blindman's buff had to stop because of an air raid.

"We can't go on this way much longer," one of the teachers muttered as we pushed into the dugout.

7

One day after inspection Miss Elson told us, "Choose two toys each. You'll have only a suitcase with you on the journey to India."

"India," Simeon said in bewilderment. "Why do we have to go to India?"

"So we don't get put in a concentration camp," Paul answered.

"I wonder if everybody's going. Wouldn't it be nice if Miss Elson stayed here to look after things."

"Good joke, Anne," I commented. "I wonder how we're getting there."

"An airplane probably," Anne said.

"An airplane!" Simeon squeaked. "But there's Japanese planes to crash us."

"Come on, Simeon." I took his hand and pushed his soft hair out of his face, like our mother used to do. "Let's go see what you can put in your green suitcase." I glanced back at Anne and shrugged, but there was a wistful look on her face which startled me. "Do you want to come, too?" She caught up with us right away.

On the last gray morning of the month, January 31, 1943, a wonky old greenish bus with cracked windows arrived at the gates of the school compound. There was no hood over the engine. As we lined up, Simeon looked in longingly, wanting to put his fingers on all those greasy old engine parts. We climbed on. The seats looked as though they'd been sat in for years and years by lots of fat people who bounced on them.

Simeon huddled in his seat and bit his nails, which were already halfway down to the little moons. "When'll we see Mummy and Daddy again?" he whispered to me.

I shrugged and stared out the window. A big crowd of Chinese children wearing blue padded jackets and pants were scrutinizing the loading of the bus. "Watch this," I whispered. I jerked up the window a bit, put my mouth near the crack, and yelled enthusiastically, "*Ting hao*. I'm a monkey. I'm a monkey," and I put up my thumb, a sign of approval in China.

Immediately they all echoed my words, grinned, and held up a forest of joyful thumbs. "*Ting hao*," very good, they yelled. "I'm a monkey."

Simeon smiled, knowing they hadn't the faintest idea what the English words meant.

"I'm a monkey."

"Ruth! Stop disgracing yourself and the whole school!" Mr. Kingsley scolded.

"I'm a monkey. I'm a monkey." The voices faded as he pushed the window closed.

I was so mad I sat back in my seat and jabbed cross looks at my shoes. Anne coughed to control her voice. I turned around, then put my head in my lap and giggled with her.

The driver hollered to his assistant, started adjusting his knobs, and bobbed his head up and down to keep an eye on the man. Starting the engine was a tricky business. His assistant engaged the crank at the front of the bus and jerked it round and round until the engine coughed, snorted, and roared. The watching children pushed back.

We hung on tight as we lurched along the narrow, cobbled streets toward the South Gate of the city.

"*Ting hao*. I'm a monkey. *Ting hao*." The Chinese children ran along beside us: older children with babies tied on their backs, smaller children yanking still smaller ones along with them.

"I wonder what they'll do," I said.

"Who?" Simeon asked.

"All those kids."

He slumped back in his seat.

Dogs barked and ran among the children's legs. Tethered chickens squawked and flapped their wings.

On the dirt road beyond the city gate was a farmer with a loudly squealing pig tied on a creaky wheelbarrow, so that its four legs pointed to the sky. The bus driver yelled and beeped at the small distracted farmer, who bumped with his pig to the side of the road and stood panting and watching as our bus lumbered past.

Simeon didn't notice.

"There are people in the rice fields." I tapped at the window but he didn't move. "I see a water buffalo. Two of them." He sighed and slid me a doleful glance.

I craned around, looking back toward the city wall. "There are three boys flying kites." I took his head in my hands and turned it, then pointed. Simeon sagged in his seat. I stopped trying and just looked for a long time.

Suddenly we stopped. "We must be there," I told

him as the driver turned off the engine. "It wasn't so long," and I got up to look.

"Ruth!" Mr. Kingsley said in a voice so cross I flopped back down in my seat.

"Aren't we there?"

"No. Of course not. We've just begun the journey."

"To the airfield?"

"We'll get to the airfield late. Now be quiet." His voice was tense and his lips were pinched.

We waited, but nothing happened. The driver and his assistant, who had been leaning forward peering out the window, slowly got off, but still nothing happened. At last I pressed my face against the glass. The road stretched like a causeway through rice fields. We had stopped a little distance from a long and sorry-looking bridge. The two men were trying to spread the higgledy-piggledy bridge planks properly across the supporting beams, but a good many planks seemed to be missing. Every now and then they'd stand up to have a look at the whole thing, perhaps trying to decide where to put the next plank. When they'd laid them as best they could, they cranked up the engine and inched the bus forward.

How will that crazy hammocky bridge hold this big busful of kids, I wondered. The front wheels rolled onto the first plank. Nobody talked. Slowly they rolled on until the whole bus was on that haphazard bridge. I looked down. Far below, foaming water raced between the steep banks. We sat still as statues. The engine groaned, the planks rattled, but the driver moved so carefully, not one flipped off. Then the front wheels touched the far side and we were over. A sigh rolled down the bus.

About a million rice fields lurched past us, and almost as many mud and thatch cottages. My nose flattened from pushing against the window, and the glass became fogged. I wiped it off and started counting roadside shrines. After eighty-three of them I got sick of it. My ears were so full of the engine racket, I started dozing like everybody else.

8

We didn't reach the airfield until evening. Mrs. Mac-Guire helped us off the high step from the bus to the ground; then Miss Elson lined us up as usual and Mr. Kingsley strode off to find out what to do with us all. When I turned to talk to Anne, she was yawning so widely I could see both her fat red tonsils. I forgot what I was going to say.

A few American soldiers wandered by and glanced at us in surprise. We were almost asleep on our feet when one young soldier with twinkly brown eyes and a cheerful grin stopped at our line, put his hands on his hips, and said, "Hey, y'all, ah'm Harry." His voice had a pleasing, unhurried sound, not what you'd expect from a soldier, but his accent puzzled us. "What'sa matter? Cat gotcha tongue?"

We watched him, baffled. "We don't call people just Harry," I told him.

"Whaddya call 'em, then?"

"Well. We could call you Uncle Harry," I suggested doubtfully.

He nodded slowly, looked solemnly down our whole line in a way that made me sure I'd said something wrong, then laughed until he lost his breath. "Never knew ah had so many kinfolk! Come on, y'all. Follow Uncle Harry."

He and another soldier led us to the toilets: first the boys vanished inside the long, low building. When they came out, doing some last-minute buttoning and buckling, they were taken to the mess hall for something to eat. We girls hesitated about going into a toilet for men. "Ah'll stay, ma'am, and see nobody goes in," Uncle Harry told Miss Elson.

Her lips drew into a thin line. "They are girls. They need a woman."

Uncle Harry shrugged. "Ah think ah best stay. In case any of the men give y'all any trouble."

Miss Elson looked icily at him. "Nobody gives me trouble."

Uncle Harry looked amused. I was dumbfounded. It looks as if he's laughing when Miss Elson talks to him like that! He is brave, I thought.

"Whatever ya say, ma'am," he said cheerfully. "But ah'll stay." He stood a little apart, hands clasped behind his back, feet astride, and pretended to inspect the sky.

We pushed open the creaky door. It was the largest outhouse I had ever seen. The double row of holes without a partition anywhere seemed to stretch for miles. We all clambered up. I took the hole nearest the door.

Through the crack I heard Uncle Harry's voice.

"Wartime flyin' ain't no picnic. Must be quite a responsibility. All them little 'uns."

"Yes. They are a burden," Miss Elson's voice snapped back.

Somebody down the line giggled nervously, afraid of falling down the hole, I suppose.

Uncle Harry's comfortable voice asked, "What'sa matter? Ya don't like kids?"

"Only an American would make such a personal remark," Miss Elson's voice said. "Likes are irrelevant. One goes where one is sent."

"Sent? Who by?" Uncle Harry sounded puzzled.

The smell in the outhouse was so strong it caught the back of your throat. Several kids started coughing.

"The directors of the mission," Miss Elson's voice answered. "All men." It sounded as if she was spitting the words at him. "Sometimes one is obliged to make the best of their mistakes." Her voice dropped as though she were talking more to herself than to Uncle Harry.

One of the girls along the row scrambled down, jerked up her knickers, and straightened her dress. "Peee-ew!"

"You sure seem like one unhappy lady," Uncle Harry said matter-of-factly.

There was no answer. But when we all creaked out the door a few minutes later, Miss Elson stood, holding her pendant and looking baffled, like someone just waking from a dream.

We watched her until she turned her head toward us. "Come now. Hurry up," she commanded.

Uncle Harry led us through the dark to the mess

hall. It was a huge Quonset hut, something like our dining room at school: long trestle tables and long benches, but four of our dining rooms could have fit into this enormous thing. The dim light left shadows all around the walls, making the room even larger. About half a dozen soldiers sat around doing nothing.

"Are we supposed to eat all this?" Simeon asked.

"Maybe it isn't for us."

"It's for y'all, honey." Uncle Harry lifted Anne onto the bench, then lifted Simeon. The rest of us scrambled up in front of the huge servings of ham, vegetables, and pudding.

"I'm too tired to eat any more." Simeon set down his empty cocoa mug, shoved the untouched plate out of the way, and laid his head on his arms.

Paul sighed and picked up the peas one at a time and ate them, too stupid with sleep to have decent manners. Anne finished nearly everything, leaving only one carrot, then began to stir her cocoa round and round, mesmerizing herself with the motion.

The room where we were to sleep was lit by one dirty light bulb which showed a row of straw mattresses on each side of the floor. Before we undressed, Mr. Kingsley and Miss Elson separated the boys from the girls by putting up a rope and safety-pinning blankets to it. There was sniffling from the other side of the blanket curtain. Then I heard, "Come on, Mole. Buck up, do."

"Aren't you scared?" I asked Anne.

"Scared of what?"

"If we might crash tomorrow?"

She thought for a minute. "Not yet I'm not. But

maybe I might be tomorrow." We untied our laces, pulled off our shoes, and set them neatly at the ends of our mattresses.

Monica gave a loud sniff, turned her back on the rest of us, and busily folded her clothes.

Suddenly I whispered, "I'm glad you're my friend."

Anne looked up in surprise and smiled. "So'm I," she whispered, and gave me a friendly push.

We got into bed. Then, through the blanket curtain, came Mr. Kingsley's voice, softer and more gentle than usual, "Boys and girls, all of you sit up now and sing with me." He waited while we slid carefully back out of our covers so they wouldn't come untucked, and then he began in his strong, deep singing voice, "God is our refuge and strength, a very present help in trouble. Therefore will not we fear. The Lord of Hosts is with us. The God of Jacob is our refuge." We lay back down and someone flicked the light switch.

The next morning after breakfast, Uncle Harry introduced us to a new soldier. "This is mah friend Milt," he told us. Milt limped badly and smoked an awful-smelling cigar. "We're gonna take y'all for a walk. Excercise all them little legs before y'all go flyin' tonight."

" 'Lo, kiddies," Milt said out of the side of his mouth. His face had the amused look most of the soldiers wore when they saw us. "Keep right up. We don't wanna lose ya." They led us past four streets of Quonset huts and groups of soldiers who all waved and called to us as if we were a parade, and past long lines of washing hung out to dry. When we reached the runway, Milt pulled his cigar out of his mouth to tell us how it had been built.

It used to be rice paddies, hundreds of them; but thousands of Chinese coolies in their umbrella-shaped bamboo hats, carrying shovels and baskets, had dug and carried for days and days, until they had a trench about a mile long and wide enough for five trucks to line up end to end across it. It was deep enough that just the coolies' heads had poked over the top. Then the coolies had started carrying in the other direction, bringing rocks and gravel and finally clay to dump into that enormous trench. When they'd smoothed the surface, even heavy bombers could take off and land. "You wouldn't of believed it unless you'd saw it with your own two eyes," Milt said.

Then Uncle Harry and Milt told us about the pilots and led us to another part of the airfield to see their fighter planes. The pilots were a swaggering lot called the Flying Tigers for good luck and because they were such aces with their P-40 airplanes. Everyone was proud of them. They knew the Japanese thought sharks meant evil, so on the noses of their planes they painted the grinning, toothy mouths of tiger sharks with bloody tongues. Just behind each propeller they made a huge round eye that watched you everywhere you went.

Even Malcolm was impressed. "I think I'd be scared, too, if one of them came flying at me. Especially if it came swooping out from behind a cloud."

"There sure are lots of them," Simeon commented, impressed by the peculiar zoo.

Milt laughed. "A good trick, most of 'em. Jist nifty decoys made of wood and canvas. We know how to fool them ol' Japs. Them's the real ones. Cain't hardly see 'em." He pointed some distance away to where the real ones stood camouflaged for protection.

At lunchtime we lined up, snickering to see so many grown men obliged to file in just like kids. They called to us from their side in their funny American: "Hi, toots," and "Howdy, pardner," and " 'Lo, sis."

Then one called, "Any gum, chum?"

"What's gumchum?" I asked. They all laughed as if they enjoyed having children around for a change.

After lunch Simeon disappeared. "Where is he?" I asked Paul. He sat on a bench, leaning against a table, staring at the door.

"Hmm?"

"Simeon. Where'd he go?"

Paul shook his head. "I don't know," he answered unhappily, and went on shaking his head. "Why's he like all this airplane stuff so much?"

"You know what Simeon wants to do when he grows up?" I asked.

Paul nodded. "He wants to have a bicycle shop and fix bicycles."

"He wants to do that all day!"

Simeon came back after a while with pockets bulging. "What've you got?" I asked.

"Special candy. Lots of special candy." He grinned and pulled out handfuls of green, yellow, and bright red cubes, not like the five counted candies we lined up to get from the locked cupboard on Sundays: those were mud brown and not much sweeter than squares of bread.

"Where'd you get it?"

"Uncle Harry." He smiled broadly. Then his forehead puckered as he went on: "He said to keep it for the airplane. I'll give you and Paul and Anne some then."

A soldier slouched by with a mop and bucket and began to slosh water across the floor. We moved to the bench by the door.

Simeon stood in front of Paul and me, smiling to himself. "Uncle Harry showed me the airplane we're going to ride on tonight," he said excitedly, "but not just the outside: the motor, and the controls, and how it works, and everything!"

"That's it, chum! Learn all you can!" a soldier said as he wiped down a table nearby. Simeon tossed him a grin.

"And look what he gave me!" His soft hair flopped on his forehead and his eyes crossed as he tried to see what he was doing. He fished inside his shirt, pulled out something on a string, and held it up for us to see, as though it were the Hope Diamond of South Africa. Several soldiers laughed, but not unkindly.

Paul stared, utterly bewildered. "What is it?"

"A butterfly nut," Simeon said dreamily. His eyes shone. "I just love motors. Daddy showed them to me at home. Just fancy! A real airplane motor! Uncle Harry even showed me where he climbs inside the wing to fix holes that shrapnel and bullets make. He has to check every single place the bullets go and then fix the holes. It's full of triangles inside the wing to hold it in the right shape. Only skinny soldiers can fit in. Skinny soldiers and little boys." He laughed with pleasure. "Boy, do I like American soldiers. I

— 62 —

hope we can go to America someday. It must be the nicest place in the world."

"It sure is that!" the soldier who'd been wiping tables said.

9

Late that afternoon as we waited in line beside the transport plane, I looked up at the huge, ugly, gray thing, wondering how Simeon could find it so fascinating. He chattered away next to me: "There's a little wire that goes all the way from a switch in the cockpit . . ." Paul hunched near him, scarcely listening.

Mr. Kingsley stood in front of us with one frowning eye, his walleye jerked to the side. Miss Elson stalked up and down. "Tie your laces, Norman. Straighten your collar, Anne." She stopped briefly next to Paul, who had pulled his sweater over most of his face so he looked like a turtle barely peeping out of its shell. "Button your coat, Paul, and put your sweater where it belongs." Her little black eyes glittered fiercely. The only time her expression softened was once when she looked at Malcolm. Mrs. MacGuire, with her wavy hair and hazel eyes, waited behind the line, and her face was kind.

"Hey, snookie! Back you get!" a soldier yelled to one of the girls who had started to wander under the airplane. I hadn't heard 'snookie' since I was at home. Suddenly I panicked. Our father's face. Our mother's face. I couldn't remember what they looked like. All I could see in my head was the black end-papers of my Bible. The photograph pasted there was blank.

But then my attention was distracted by one soldier who broke away from a cluster of men and walked thoughtfully toward us. "My name is Keith LaFontaine," he said. "I'll be flying you to Kunming, so I'd like to meet each of you before we take off." His dark eyes were very serious, but he smiled a bit. He came down the line, listened carefully as we told him our names, and stopped to shake hands with each one of us, making us feel we were important to him. When he came to Anne he stopped and looked at her as if recognizing her from somewhere.

She smiled up at him. "Anne," she said, "Anne Langdon."

A strange expression crossed his face, almost as though he was going to cry. "My little girl has red hair," he said, and rested his hand on her curls.

In the distance I saw somebody running toward us and squinted. "Hey, Simeon, look who's coming," I said.

Uncle Harry stopped at the top of the line. "Ya'll forgot the tangerines," he panted and walked down the line giving us each one from his basket. "Suck the sections when the plane goes up. It'll help your ears."

"I've got my candy," Simeon said when Uncle Harry reached him.

"Ya wanna go easy on that. Too much'll make ya sick."

Milt, who had been busy doing something or other, limped over. "Hey, chief, the coolies brought some extry cans o' gas. D'you want 'em?"

Keith LaFontaine frowned. "It's in mighty short supply, but I guess as long as they're here it's better to have too much than too little."

The coolies swarmed onto the wings with the oblong tins of gasoline and dumped them into the fuel tank. When they were finished a couple of soldiers started shouting; two more ran to the propellers and pushed them around. Before we knew it, we were lifted up and fastened into bucket seats along either side of the purring airplane.

"Don't be scared," Simeon said, and happily gave me two of his candies, a red one and a yellow one. Putting his hand on Paul's knee, he said, "Cheer up, Ratty," and dropped several candies into his hand; then he popped two into his own mouth. Suddenly his face turned white. He clenched his teeth, sat on his hands, and nearly choked on the candy.

The engines burst into a roar which grew louder and louder as if leading up to an explosion. All that separated us from the full blast of those engines was a sheet of aluminum so thin it could be pierced with a screwdriver.

Mr. Kingsley stood with his head bowed and his lips praying, but we couldn't hear a thing his lips said. He sat down quickly and fastened his belt. The airplane catapulted down the runway. We lurched toward the tail. Suddenly our stomachs took a nose dive as we were slung up into the air, shaken, and jerked as if the plane were trying to get rid of us. Anne and Monica both turned whiter and whiter and started vomiting. Paul looked pretty miserable. Simeon sat with his head dropped forward. His hands clutched the rod which held the front of the bucket seats.

Then finally everything settled. The sky grew black and we dozed a bit.

I pushed my hand into my coat pocket and felt something warm and round: the tangerine! I hadn't needed it because of Simeon's candy. It was comforting to hold, and made me think of Uncle Harry's funny story about learning to fly planes in America.

"One day some of ma buddies and me decided we'd have us a little fun," he told us. "We took off the door of this here practice plane and went up."

Simeon's eyes almost popped out. "You mean you flew with no door on? No door at all!"

"Yeh-ah. That's what we did. Then we lay on the floor when we was up and looked outa the door, peekin' way down at them purty green trees all the way down."

"Weren't you scared?" I asked.

"Na. We was young an' foolish. Then ah took this here orange outa ma pocket and told ma buddies t'watch. What a purty sight: that orange arcin' down over all that green."

I held my tangerine more firmly and squirmed around to look toward *our* airplane door. Very carefully I scrutinized the curved, shadowy oblong. A bar about the length of my arm latched the door. I *thought* it was properly closed. Suddenly a darker shadow swept across it, making it seem to move. The door's falling off, I thought!

I was so scared I tried to find something else to

look at. In front of me was the pile of luggage, well roped to the floor. I tried to guess which suitcase belonged to which kid, and hunted for names painted on them. One black case had a large sticker of an ocean steamer. But it jiggled so badly I got dizzy looking at it and closed my eyes. Without meaning to, I fell asleep.

At one crazy lurch my eyes opened a crack and saw Mr. Kingsley looking at Miss Elson in the dirty light of the one bulb. He pointed up, to God, I guess, because there wasn't anything else. From the caged light bulb snowflakes seemed to fall, slowly at first, then faster, and more of them. It made me chilly but was soft and light. A fire began right in front of me. I lurched forward. Miss Elson held a flashlight. Syrupy-headed and scared, I blurted out, "O God, don't let us crash!"

Suddenly out of nowhere there was a brief, brilliant light. We hit something so hard that if we hadn't been fastened down we'd have been thrown into the cockpit with the pilot. The plane bounced high in the air, banged and bounced and roared for an hour or more, or so it seemed, though it was only about ten minutes.

Simeon and Paul frantically pressed their ears. I was too terrified to do anything.

The roar stopped.

In the sudden quiet and gloom the teachers moved back and forth looking like corpses, unfastening us. The only sound was the *click click click* of the buckles. We were lifted from the airplane onto the ground. A flashlight spotlighted each child.

Even Keith LaFontaine had to be helped off the

airplane, his legs were so wobbly. He sat right down on the ground and dropped his head on his knees. He was crying.

"Lily-livered jerk," an airfield man muttered.

"Wait a minute. You see his cargo?" our other pilot asked.

"Yeah. Kids."

"The Jap raid on your airfield kept us circling until the tanks were almost dry."

The man swore, then mumbled an apology in our direction.

"Those tanks would have been empty, but the coolies at our end made a mistake and brought us extra gas." He started toward us and almost bumped into Miss Elson.

"Children, line up here," she commanded, just as if it were time for inspection. She got us ready shortly before a truck arrived. We didn't know where we were, or what time it was, or where the truck was taking us; and it's funny, but it was oddly comforting to hear Miss Elson snap out the same old order as if we were actually back at school.

10

Anne and I peeked out of the closet where we'd spent the night. A makeshift line of mattresses stretched end to end down the hall, with a lane just wide enough for our feet to pass beside them. Odds and ends of blankets covered the girls, who were beginning to wriggle and stir and raise their heads to look about. More heads poked out of two more doorways. A brief squabble erupted down the line, then ended in giggles. We stood on the mattresses to dress, straightened the blankets as best we could, and streamed into a room where we took turns standing at tables to eat.

For some reason, during the next three days there was only one air raid. But there was no school, nothing to play on, and hardly a stick to turn into a doll. The teachers and missionaries were busy and preoccupied, probably trying to figure out how to get us all from Kunming to Calcutta. We grew bored and cross.

Paul, who loved boring times, was quite cheerful. Simeon moped loyally about after him. But on the third day the two of them started acting like a couple of conspirators. They made several trips to the back of the mission house, glancing suspiciously about.

I wondered what they were up to and followed them at a distance. Around the end of the rambly old building, the boys crouched to the ground beside a leafless bush near the compound wall; but I couldn't see exactly what they were doing. Skulking like a cat after a bird, I got about two paces from them when they sensed somebody was near. Slowly they turned their heads. Paul smiled. "You won't tell, will you?"

On the ground between the two boys sat a coppery-green pigeon with a lavender breast and red feet. One wing drooped at a funny angle. "What's the matter with it?" I asked.

Simeon fed it a little of the rice in his fist. "Its wing's a bit broken," he said. From the other side of the wall came the sound of other pigeons gurgling and cooing.

I leaned against the wall, idly watching. Presently I noticed a little hole where the mortar had fallen out between two bricks which had begun to crumble. I looked through. "There's an orchard on the other side of the wall. Must be nice in spring," I told the boys.

"Let's see." Simeon got up and peeked. "I can't see anything, but there's something glittery."

"Something glittery?" Then I whispered, "I think it's an eye."

"An eye?"

"Sssh. It's an eye."

Paul got up. "It blinked."

A voice said, "What you do?"

We didn't say a word.

The voice said again, "What you do?"

Simeon put his mouth near the hole. "We're taking care of a pigeon."

"Pigeon!" the voice exclaimed. The orchard appeared again through the hole. There was a sound of scrambling and a tree branch bounced. Over the top of the wall the head of a thirteen- or fourteen-year-old Chinese boy appeared and looked down at us. "Is pigeon of Father!" the boy said anxiously. "I bring pigeon to Father."

Paul and Simeon looked at each other, then at me. "If Paul gets on my shoulders . . ." I said slowly.

"Wait!" The boy's head disappeared. There was a sound of running.

The pigeon looked at us with its round, surprised eyes. "You must be some pigeon," Paul commented.

The footsteps were slower as they came back, and there was a sound of something dragging and then scraping up the side of the wall. The top of a light bamboo ladder appeared. "I drop," the boy's voice called. The ladder jerked up, wobbled on the top of the wall, then slipped over. Simeon and I grabbed it.

The boy's head appeared again. "Carry pigeon!" he commanded. Cradling the pigeon in his arm, Paul carefully climbed up. "Come!" the boy said, and pointed to Simeon. He glanced back at me, then began to climb. When he reached the top of the wall, I set my foot on the first rung. "Girl no!"

I looked up in consternation. "But they'll come back?"

"Yes. Yes. No afraid." The boy grabbed the top rung and pulled up the ladder. There was more scraping as he slid it down the other side of the wall. I looked through the hole but I couldn't see where they were going. Their footsteps and the sound of dragging grew fainter and fainter. I waited for ten, maybe fifteen minutes, but they didn't show up. Before long Anne came out.

"What'll you do?" she asked when she'd heard. She peered through the hole. "It looks like a very rich man's garden."

I shook my head. "Dunno." I wasn't exactly scared, but I didn't know what to do.

We heard calling.

At the front of the mission home we found a few

kids, mostly boys, clustered in an excited group. Since it was foggy enough to be fairly safe from air raids, two of the missionaries had decided to take us out for a walk on the streets. Mr. Baer was a big, comfortable man with three or four chins and a deep, rumbly laugh that cheered us up even though we didn't understand all his jokes. He clutched his head in both hands, shook it, and moaned, "The hosts of the children of Israel have descended like locusts upon us." When we snickered uncertainly, he winked; we laughed properly. A few more boys joined us.

Mrs. Baer was like a doll that's too special to play with: small and very pretty. Their plan was to take us out right away.

"Now, I must number this host I have before me." Mr. Baer began counting, but he started, "A thousand and one, a thousand and two . . ."

"Alfred!" his wife said, half laughing.

"A thousand and eleven, a thousand and twelve. Now, where are the rest? Surely we are missing . . ."

There was an imperious banging on the gate of the compound and a loud commanding, "*Wei! Wei!*" The gatekeeper stumbled out of his little house, which was built into the wall next to the gate, and shuffled sleepily to the wicket. He slid back the bolt of this small door and peered through. Immediately he jerked back, closed the wicket, and hollered for his wife. Briskly they started work on the fastenings of the great gate, which was solid black, as high as the roofs of the houses, and wide enough for a truck to pass. Pushing with all their might and main, they heaved open the whole great gate, then stepped to the side, bowing obsequiously.

Mr. Baer's mouth dropped open. Several more kids ran up and craned forward with the rest of us.

On the street stood a very impressive soldier, who must have been a general at least. His uniform was meticulously clean and pressed, with lots of gleaming buttons; his hat, belt, and polished shoes were new. On one side of him stood Simeon, on the other stood Paul, and behind them jostled an expectant crowd.

The general looked stiffly at Mr. Baer and opened his mouth to speak. Then he caught sight of Averell, Norman, and half a dozen more boys peeking out from behind Mr. Baer. He glanced down at Simeon and Paul, and again at the rest of the boys. A look of awe spread over his face. "These . . . these are all your sons?" he asked in amazement.

"Yes. No," Mr. Baer answered, very flustered. The general must have thought Mr. Baer had an awful lot of concubines to have so many sons about the same age. "But those boys . . ." Mr. Baer pointed. "They belong here. I hope they haven't offended you."

"No, no. Not so. They brought me back my Imperial Pigeon. I wish to present my thanks." The general pushed the two boys forward, bowed, and left.

For a minute Mr. Baer looked down in perplexity at Simeon and Paul. They glanced up and grinned. "You want to see what he gave us?"

Mr. Baer herded them back into the compound and motioned for the gate to be closed; already the crowd had grown. Paul held up a bronze chain with a small green jade cameo of a pigeon in flight. Simeon held up his chain with a disk about the size of the rim of a Chinese teacup. It looked like milky glass until he held it to the light, when an amber moon appeared, but not a full moon. "He has lots of kinds of pigeons," Simeon explained.

"And he always carries two or three homing pigeons when he travels to take letters to his son," Paul went on.

"But the Imperial Pigeon is his favorite. Their family's been raising them for a long time." Simeon dropped the moonstone disk inside his shirt. It clinked against his butterfly nut. Half a dozen more kids dashed toward us.

"Wonders will never cease," Mr. Baer said. "That man has never spoken to any missionary. They always say if you want a key to open any door in China, take a child with you." Mr. Baer stood for a few minutes, shaking his head. "Take partners. Get in line." We formed our crocodile. "Beyond the gates, you must obey me immediately," he said. "No pointing. No wandering off. All stay together." He let his words sink in. Then in his holiday voice he said, "Ready? Forward march!"

We walked along the crowded, bumpy street, past all the little shops, but there were too many of us to buy anything. "You'd need a rickshaw load of money to buy for this host, and I'm not provided with that!" Mr. Baer threw out his hands, which made it seem we were indeed a great and mighty throng.

"Don't you wish he was one of our teachers?" I whispered.

"Mmmm hmm." Anne nodded emphatically.

Crowds of inquisitive little children followed us, many carrying the usual baby brothers and sisters tied on their backs. "Foreign devil! Foreign devil!" they chanted together. "Big nose! Big nose!"

Clusters of Chinese soldiers were everywhere. They wore padded tan jackets, mostly patched and faded; loose wrinkled pants, long strips of cloth wrapped around their legs, and straw sandals. Their equipment hung from their belts: an enamel rice bowl and mug, and a toothbrush. Some carried glittering bayonets on straps over their shoulders.

"Can you imagine jabbing one of those into somebody?" Anne whispered to me. I started and shivered. Somehow it was very different seen from the top of the mulberry tree at home.

We pressed back as a convoy of American military trucks rolled slowly through the street. "Yoo hoo, kiddies! This ain't no place for little squirts like you!" a soldier called.

We turned down a side street. "Now what do you think about this?" Mr. Baer and Simeon stopped, and all the rest of us bumped together to watch two pigs fighting and grunting over some old green cabbage leaves, just like the pigs the lost boy watched in the old Bible times. A little distance from them an opium addict lay asleep—he didn't want to fight anymore about anything.

When his turn was finished and it was time for someone else to hold Mr. Baer's hand, Simeon meandered down the line to be Paul's partner again.

"I wonder if we could train a pigeon to carry letters for us," Paul said.

"Hmm?" Simeon looked puzzled for a minute. "Oh. Yes. Isn't Mr. Baer the nicest man? I think he's the nicest man in Kunming. I wish he'd come with us."

Paul said, "That big boy said his father was going to let him train two homing pigeons."

Simeon said, "Maybe Mr. and Mrs. Baer would come with us instead of Mr. Kingsley and Miss Elson."

Paul said, "I thought those fruit pigeons were pretty, those pale green feathers with the black." The two of them walked along carrying on two totally separate conversations.

Our crocodile wound past coffin makers, filigree silversmiths, shoemakers, embroiderers, and stopped near an umbrella shop where an old man, his son, and his grandson hunched over their work. Mr. Baer decided to count us again before we crossed the street. He walked along the line patting shoulders until he came to Paul. "Where's Simeon?" Paul looked perplexed, then lifted his hand and stared as though Simeon should be holding it. "Think, Paul. Where is Simeon?" He put his hands on Paul's shoulders as if to steady him while he thought.

Slowly Paul shook his head, very troubled, still staring into his cupped hand. "He was here. We were talking about the pigeons."

Mr. Baer told us all to turn around as he walked to the tail of the line. "We'll have to go back the way we've come."

I felt as though my heart were bumping along the paving stones when each place we looked Simeon wasn't there.

Anne gave my hand a squeeze. "Don't worry. He'll probably turn up soon."

"Don't worry!" I answered sarcastically. "That's what you say. You don't even have a brother. You don't know."

"That's what you think," she said, almost under her breath. Her tone of voice made me glance at her, but her face was turned away.

Suddenly I heard a man talking in our dialect instead of Kunming Chinese, which was hard to understand. I jerked to a stop and stood on tiptoe, looking all around. A military truck rolled by, briefly blocking my view.

"Stop! Mr. Baer, stop! I see him. I see Simeon!" I yelled. He was sitting on a little counter across the street talking with a lantern maker. I almost started crying. "Simeon," I said when we'd gotten past the people, the rickshaws, and the trucks, "how long've you been lost here?"

He looked down at us all. "I wasn't lost! I was here!" Nobody knew what to answer. "Look what Mr. Chen makes, and he talks our kind of Chinese, and he even looks like our cook at home." Mr. Chen did look like our cook: jolly eyes, and bald head, shiny as a brass pot. He smiled and nodded to everybody.

The lantern he was building had children skipping in front of a sun which slowly rose and set as the pictures turned. They were painted on a paper drum attached to a rod. At the top of the rod was a wooden propeller. The heat of the two candles made the propeller at the top of the lantern slowly turn inside a fixed outer frame of windows. That's what had caught Simeon's eye when we walked past.

Almost right away a crowd collected, pushing so close to see what was happening that we could hardly move.

A couple of American soldiers caught in the jam craned forward. "English kids!" they yelled. "Lots of them. My God! Where'd they come from?" Several of their buddies waded through the crowds and joined them.

Somebody behind me began to feel my dress collar for the quality of the cloth. I jerked free. I was really angry. "You dummy, Simeon," I shouted, "why'd you go off like this, scaring us all to bits."

The Chinese tittered and pointed at the foreign child who was making such an improper racket.

The American soldiers guffawed. "That's it, girlie! You tell him!"

Mrs. Baer put her kind hand on my shoulder. "It's all right, little mother. The lost is found." Her husband bowed to Mr. Chen, lifted Simeon down, and shouted for the way to be cleared.

"Mr. Baer, when do we have to go on that other airplane?" Simeon asked, suddenly anxious.

"Maybe tonight."

11

We clambered over the high threshold of the small door in the great double gate. Our suitcases were heaped up just inside. I didn't know whether to be excited or scared.

Hurriedly we washed for an early supper. The first relay stood at the table to eat while the rest waited, chewing fingernails, or squinting anxiously, or nibbling on the cuffs of sweaters. Miss Elson's face was pinched into frowning columns of creases. "Hurry up, children. No dallying. No more talking. Eat up," she said. We bolted our food.

Just as we finished, a convoy of military trucks rumbled past the walls. "You hear that?" I asked Simeon. "It's trucks, lots of them full of soldiers."

"I know. They're taking people away." He looked toward Mr. Baer. "Then they'll take us away." He chewed on the end of his pocketknife, then jammed that in his pocket and started on his fingernails.

"We're not going to a concentration camp."

"I know."

"We're leaving all that."

"I know."

"Come on, Simeon. We're going on another airplane. Isn't it exciting?" I said with stupid, phony encouragement.

He just looked at me.

Outside the closed gate more trucks rumbled and stopped. Truck doors slammed. "Open up! Open up!" several American voices shouted.

"Children! Line up!" Miss Elson's command rounded us up in no time.

The gatekeeper and his wife hustled about, quarreling with each other as they heaved open the gate. We craned forward, trying to see through the widening crack. Four American soldiers and a couple of very noisy weapons-carrier trucks waited for us on the street, surrounded by a large crowd of Chinese children.

"Howdy, kids!" one soldier shouted. An American flag was tattooed on the back of his right hand. "Ready for a little spin down the road?" We looked at Miss Elson and smiled uncertainly. "Careful how you toss 'em in, Fred," he called to a whiskery soldier. They backed the first truck into the compound.

"Easy does it." Fred lifted up Anne. "Carrots, eh?" he commented, gently touching one of her red curls with his stubby finger. "Upsy-daisy. Here we go." He had a funny comment for each of us.

Miss Elson stood near the truck, eyeing us. She kept lifting her hand as though to finger her pendant, but it was buttoned inside her coat.

Simeon cried. I guess the soldiers reminded him of Uncle Harry. He rubbed his fists in his eyes, but the tears kept coming.

Miss Elson snapped, "It's been a difficult matter to arrange this journey. You're a most fortunate little boy to be able to go where it's safe. Look at the poor Chinese children who have to stay here. Dry your eyes. You do have your handkerchief?"

Simeon nodded and carefully pulled his hanky from his pocket, unfolded it, wiped his nose, and sat down on the wooden bench at the side of the truck.

The Chinese children, in their blue quilted jackets and pants, were having a high old time. As the trucks started moving they ran alongside pointing and yelling, "Big nose! Big nose!"

"*Ting hao!* Big nose!" one little girl called, and blew a kiss, as she had learned from the American soldiers.

"*Ting hao!* Little nose!" Anne and I shouted, and blew kisses back to her with both hands.

"*Ting hao.*" The little girl poked a couple of her friends. They all giggled, blowing kisses as they ran, and almost stumbled.

The weather began to clear; it was more like a picnic than a war journey. The trucks tickled and joggled us over the cobbled streets, through the city gate, and over the deeply corrugated road. Their engines revved up to top gear, then shifted to the *nyeh* of slowing down. We mimicked all those truck-engine sounds until even Simeon joined the fun.

Near the airfield the trucks suddenly jolted to a standstill. A scattering of Chinese soldiers stood on the road angrily waving their arms high over their heads in a Stop! Stop! Stop! motion. Mr. Kingsley jumped out of the truck with the drivers. The soldiers scowled and hollered, angrily pointing at an American transport plane on the airstrip. But one man kept bobbing above the others, shaking his head, jerking a piece of paper, and shrieking, "*Bu! Bu! Bu!*" No! No! No! Gesticulating to right and left, he informed everybody, as though he were a top commander, that we were *not* to go on that American Air Force plane. We were expected to use one belonging to the Chinese National Airlines. These were the orders of Generalissimo Chiang Kai-shek.

The Generalissimo was a familiar face: his picture was everywhere, proudly looking out over the tops of people's heads, as if he wanted no argument from anyone about anything.

Mr. Kingsley seemed more and more puzzled. "The Chinese National Airlines?" he asked finally. "But we did inquire. They informed us nothing was available."

"You are to wait for one." The man shook his paper threateningly in Mr. Kingsley's face.

"How long will that be?"

"I do not know. But this I do know. You are to wait."

At last Mr. Kingsley turned and hopelessly shook his head. The trucks lumbered around, scattering the soldiers like chickens, and took us back to the city.

That night we lay on the mattresses in our clothes. I dreamed a strange dream of hundreds of children dressed in blue, children from our school and from the streets, all laughing and blowing kisses to one another. But suddenly the bombers' moon rose and a bitter wind blew from it, blowing us apart and away. I woke up. My blanket had slipped to the floor and I was cold and scared.

The next day dragged by. There was nothing to do but wander irritably around. The pigeon was gone. Simeon kicked the nest apart while the rest of us watched. "Dumb pigeon, even if you are Imperial," he grumbled, then peeked through the hole, but saw nothing of the boy. He spent the rest of the day moping.

After supper Mr. Kingsley gave us a lecture so serious his cheek twitched and his walleye jerked. "There is to be no noise. No talking. No whispering. Nothing," he said in a voice like a gun. "If just one of you disobeys, it could send us all back." You could have heard a grain of rice tick to the floor. "And we don't know how long it would take to arrange something else." He said the last word of each sentence with his teeth bared, as though he were biting it out of the air.

We formed a silent line. The soldiers acted funny: not a word, not a greeting, not even a wink as they lifted us into their trucks.

The main sound as we were driven through the empty streets was the echoing roar of the truck engines. It was later and darker than the night before. Mr. Kingsley got precariously to his feet. Clinging to the top of the truck, he motioned for us all to lie flat. We slid off the benches and onto the floor. I tilted my head a bit to peek up. Mr. Kingsley still stood wobbling, his finger across his lips. Then he slid to the floor and crouched below the tailgate. Our faces bumped against the cold, hard metal.

Suddenly we stiffened. Chinese soldiers shouted at one another on the road. They'll see us! I thought. They'll peer right in the back of this truck and see our white faces. I gritted my teeth and made fists, wanting terribly to lift my head and look. Anne's curls brushed my cheek. I felt for Simeon's hand and held it tight. Very slowly the trucks rolled forward, crunching over the packed dirt road. We passed one bunch of yelling soldiers. But the wheels kept rolling. Another bunch.

Then, before we could figure out what was going on, we were thrown back against Mr. Kingsley as the trucks leaped forward, engines roaring, throttles wide open.

In a few minutes the trucks slammed on their brakes without even slowing down. We were thrown in the opposite direction, against one another in a heap. Chains rattled; bolts grated; the tailgate dropped open. A new roar sounded, louder and stronger than the truck engines. Soldiers' arms reached in and grabbed us, lifting us along a line of men and high into the open door of a shuddering airplane. Lift. Dump. Lift. Dump. We landed in a confused huddle against the pile of luggage.

Swiftly the teachers fastened us in. Dirty smoke swept past the many little windows. All at once bright flames streaked through the smoke and the airplane shot forward, bounced hard, and swooped up, leaving us far behind. Or so it felt. I gripped the front bar of the seat with all my might and main. I felt like a dried bean in a tin can kicked down the road.

Finally the worst of the bouncing settled. We swallowed repeatedly to keep our ears from popping as the plane climbed. The smell of gasoline, oil, and vomit clogged the air. We drooped back in our seats. On the floor space between us was the pile of luggage, well roped to secure it. I could see the brass corners of Simeon's case. I poked him and pointed. But he had all he could do to keep from retching.

The luggage and the other kids slowly grew blurry, and my eyes shut.

Although I was fat with sweaters and a coat, I was niggled awake by the coldness in my hands and feet. I hunched over my knees, trying to get warm. The caged bulb overhead cast a thin light on everything. I glanced up at Simeon, and leaned closer, right in his face. He looked awful, gray and pinched as old rubber. I grabbed his shoulders tight and tried to jiggle him, but he gasped and choked.

"Mrs. MacGuire, come quick!" I yelled, but my voice didn't carry to her. He's dying, I know he's dying, I thought, and took his hand. It was limp and cold. Mrs. MacGuire wobbled and swayed down the row toward us, shining her flashlight into each face. Twice she stopped and did something. When she came to Simeon she set a small tank on the floor, then held a mask over his nose and mouth, fiddled with the straps to buckle them, and looked intently at him. As always when she was working hard, she pressed her lips tight together in a thin, determined line. Suddenly her face let go. She patted his shoulder, gave me a busy little smile, and moved on. I let out my breath in a noisy sigh of relief.

Simeon, with his mask strapped to his head, dozed and shivered on my right; Anne bumped heads with me on my left as we drowsed forward and dragged back.

Suddenly we jerked awake. The wings of the airplane grated as though being wrenched apart. The engine blasted our ears. We struck the ground hard and were thrown back and forth as the plane bounced, went on roughly bouncing, then stopped.

Silence.

"Did we crash?" I whispered to Mrs. MacGuire.

"No."

"Then are we there? Is this Calcutta?"

"No. This is Assam. We'll get off for a stretch while they're refueling. There's still quite a way to go." She unbuckled Simeon's mask.

"Why'd he have to wear that thing?"

"We were flying so high he couldn't breathe without extra oxygen. About twenty thousand feet, they told us, to get over the Himalayan Mountains."

"Is that why we bounced so much? Going over the tops of those mountains?"

"No. That was wind." She gave a little shudder. "But we're past that now, thank God."

On the ground Anne and I turned to face each other, struggling to straighten our backs, but we were so stiff we almost yelped as we put our hands on each other's shoulders and slowly unbent. Her face looked bleached in the glimmer of the starlight.

"Walk around. Walk around now while you can," Miss Elson ordered. Anne and I took turns staying with Simeon, who hunched in a miserable little heap.

"Ruth, that's far enough." Miss Elson's voice hooked me back. "Stay with the rest. Don't wander off."

"Why's she think we're always trying to do the wrong thing? Why's she always make us feel we've done something bad?" I whispered angrily to Anne.

"She's just an old meany. Don't worry about her."
Anne put her arm around my shoulders.

". . . thirty-five, thirty-six. Move up. Move up.
Thirty-seven, thirty-eight . . ." Again we were lifted
into the plane.

"What a stink!" Anne pinched her nose and settled back into her seat.

The plane droned on and on. Just as we began to
think the journey would never end, we banged to a
stop and the door of the airplane swung open. It felt
as if we'd landed in a soggy, floodlit laundry room
on the hottest day of the summer. Our sweaters and
coats prickled. The brilliant sunshine of the Calcutta
airfield made us squint.

12

Anne found a big Rowntree's Chocolate tin with a
lid, for catching the crickets. She set it on the ground
between us and lifted up a rock so slowly her face
turned crimson in the heat of the Calcutta afternoon.
"There's one! Quick! Catch it!" I caught it and poked
it in. One jumped out. "There's some more." I caught
two and poked them in. One jumped out. "How
many are there now?" Anne asked.

"How can I count them? Every time we put more
in, more jump out."

"Let me listen." She put the tin to her ear. "Not
too many. I can only hear a few clicking."

Slowly we worked our way down the tall iron fence of the Royal Calcutta Rowing Club, where we were staying until arrangements were completed for the next part of our journey. Already it had been two weeks. We were only faintly interested in our next move: it was nice to stay in such a beautiful place.

"Bluebells, cockleshells, eeny-iny over," several girls sang for their jump-rope game on the wide lawn.

"Want to play?" Megan called.

"No."

"What're you doing?" she asked crossly. "Why do you two always have to do something different?"

"We just don't want to play." I put the tin to my ear. "Better get some more crickets."

Seven crickets later we had worked our way down to where Simeon hunkered beside the fence, where he spent most of his time. Paul sat patiently beside him, passing the time watching the crowds which pushed by all day.

"They look as if they've had a war here," he commented as a bony old man limped past. He had only one leg and a chunk of wood strapped to the stump of the other. Behind him straggled several men and two women—arms, legs, ears were missing. Half of one man's face was caved in.

"It's a wonder those coolies aren't squashed flat with those gigantic bundles on their heads," I said, and pointed.

Suddenly the crowd parted as though a siren had sounded. Down the space ambled a white cow. It sampled a tray of oranges, a basket of eggplant, nosed through the garbage at the side of the street, then knocked a cabbage out of a basket. It rolled a little way before the cow could bite it.

"I wonder why they don't stop that cow," Paul said.

"Mr. Kingsley said they think it's holy, so it can do what it likes," I told him.

A boy about our age, with knobbly elbows and ribs that showed through his ragged shirt, poked his begging hand through the fence. "Baksheesh?" he inquired. Three more small hands poked through lower down. "Baksheesh?" But we had nothing to put in them. Anne and I backed up, embarrassed.

"Simeon." I clutched his wrist. "Come help us. You're good at this."

"Good at what?" Slowly he turned around.

"Catching crickets."

"What for?"

"That doesn't matter. Just help us."

"I'll help you catch crickets," he answered suspiciously, "but that's all." He got up and started toward a new pile of stones. Paul turned back to watch. "Here's a bunch," Simeon called, and held his hands cupped together, then slid the crickets into the tin as Anne opened the lid a crack. "They can't breathe with that lid on."

"How can we keep them in, then?"

"D'you have some string? You could use this." He held out his handkerchief.

Carefully we set the tin with the hanky tied over it at the foot of a mimosa tree and heaped stones around it to conceal it.

"What's it for?" Simeon asked again, very suspicious.

"Don't worry," Anne said.

"I'm tired of skipping rope. Let's play air raids," somebody hollered. They made the shrieks of the sirens and the boom of the planes, racing round and round the lawn.

Anne asked, "You want to go play air raids with them now, Simeon?"

"No!" he answered, almost angrily.

Anne and I got up just after the sun, held our breath, and tiptoed outside so quietly nobody knew we were gone.

"Which tree was it?" Anne whispered in my ear.

"Over there."

"Look! Look quick!" She pointed to the top of the palm grove, where two monkeys were swinging along. They leaped neatly to the ledge of a window which had been left temptingly open and disappeared. We walked as quickly as we could to the mimosa tree and found our crickets.

"There's a bunch more! Let's add some fresh ones." We unknotted the string, slid back the handkerchief, and hurried several crickets into the tin. Quickly we walked back to the club.

We hesitated on the threshold and glanced around at the gleaming tables and heavily curtained windows. The dining room of the Royal Calcutta Rowing Club did not invite tricks. We sneaked by the first row of portraits. One young officer took his duties very seriously: his finger pointed as though to a "Thou shalt not . . ." We hurried past him. Near the next window an older, more genial officer hung. If you walked past him a little beyond the table, one eye always winked.

We caught our breath, swallowed like frogs, and gingerly set the tin at Miss Elson's place without making even a tick, then clapped our hands over our mouths to hold the giggles and crept back to bed.

The breakfast bell rang. Simeon stood behind his high-backed chair at Mrs. MacGuire's table, as far from Miss Elson as he could get.

"Come on," I whispered to Anne. "We gotta be close to see the fun."

"Not too close."

". . . and we thank Thee for Miss Elson's diligent attention to duty, her care for all these, Thy little ones . . ." Mr. Kingsley's birthday prayer went on and on.

I began to lose my appetite. I peeked at Anne, whose eyes were still properly closed. Our present gave several clicks. I poked her. She made an I-don't-care face.

". . . for all Thy bountiful mercies to us. Amen."

We sat down. Miss Elson looked at her three presents: a pale blue one, a lumpy brown one, and a white one which clicked, all reflected in the highly polished table. She smiled a little. When we had sung "Happy Birthday," she opened her pale blue present of six candies a good kid must have got from an American soldier. Miss Elson said, "Thank you, Monica."

Then she picked up the lumpy present, slid off a

rather grubby bit of string, and spread back the paper. She swallowed several times and fingered her pendant.

"You'll wear it, won't you," Malcolm said eagerly. "I know it's not terribly good, but I polished it smooth." He gave her one of his sudden smiles.

Miss Elson looked happily at him. "My brother carved me one years ago." She put the wooden ring on her smallest finger. It only just fit. "Thank you, Malcolm." He settled back in his chair.

Then Miss Elson took the handkerchief off Anne's and my present. Her expression went flat. A crowd of crickets hopped gaily out. Several jumped into our porridge and got stuck. Two or three sprang into our mugs of milk. Five sank in the jam. The rest leaped and skidded about, seeming to multiply because of the sharp reflections in the tabletop.

Mr. Kingsley cleared his throat; a sliver of a smile slipped across his face, then left him as stern as ever. I wondered briefly if he'd done anything naughty when he was a kid.

Mrs. MacGuire gasped and looked troubled. Simeon sat beside her, eating around the edge of his porridge without looking up, except through the corners of his eyes.

It got so quiet we could hear the tick of the last crickets scrambling out. I looked down and felt for Anne's comforting hand under the table.

But Miss Elson's eyes stared like stones. Her mouth tightened. "I see there are children who take advantage of birthdays for their own selfish ends. Everyone suffers for it."

Suffering, I thought, what suffering?

"Collect the crickets."

Unless she means not eating porridge. We sure have different ideas about suffering.

"Hurry up. Take them outside."

Better not look at Anne, I thought. We're sure to laugh and give ourselves away.

"Get them out of the milk and jam."

We collected the sticky crickets and the wet ones. Miss Elson sat back down and passed around the bread.

How can she look as though absolutely nothing happened—nothing good, nothing bad? Then I almost choked on my bread. I couldn't believe Anne and I had been so dumb. Miss Elson held up the hanky and shook it. Simeon's red laundry number 62 showed.

Later at inspection she said, "Simeon, where is your handkerchief?"

He looked at his toes and mumbled something.

"Look at me, Simeon. Where is your handkerchief?"

The inspection line was so quiet we could hear the ceiling-fan motor. All that moved was Simeon's soft hair in the breeze. Reluctantly he looked up. "It was on the crickets," he whispered.

She gave him his hanky neatly folded. "Next." Paul's blue eyes looked very startled. "Next," she said again, more sharply, and he moved forward as if in a dream. I suppose he couldn't believe his friend had helped with such a prank.

"Next." Averell moved up.

"Next." Monica moved up.

"Next." I slunk up. She yanked me out of line and pushed me to the side until inspection was over. She did the same to Anne.

She always knows, I thought.

Everyone stared curiously at us, realizing we must have done something new and dreadful.

There was quite a row, which ended, "Never do that again."

We went outside. I told Simeon in an admiring voice, "You didn't tell, even though we got you in trouble."

"You're a jolly good sport," Anne added.

Simeon smiled shyly and stayed contentedly with us until Paul meandered out. But neither of them laughed the way Anne and I did every time we saw a cricket jump.

That night, when everyone else was asleep, I lay in bed and stared at the faint shadow of the fan on the ceiling. The low flame of the kerosene lamp flickered every now and then and made the shadow waver. Miss Elson's soldier steps sounded in the hall, followed by Mrs. MacGuire's near-shuffle. They stopped at the end of our temporary dormitory.

"Have you ever felt such heat, Florence?" Mrs. MacGuire said. She flapped her handkerchief a few times at her face.

"I visited London once when they said you could fry an egg on the pavement."

"Poor London. I wonder how they're doing with all that terrible bombing."

"Father lives there now. But he never writes. I don't suppose I'll know until the war is done what's become of him." Miss Elson sounded bitter. They walked on to the boys' dormitory.

Hardly any presents for her birthday, no letters, hardly any kids liking her: I wondered if anything pleasant ever happened to her. Then I remembered: we had been playing on the swings at school when a brisk, sandy-haired Englishman came through the gate. He walked like the wind toward Miss Elson, who was on duty outside, and spoke to her. She smiled and chatted with him up the path to the school building. We all looked at each other, unable to believe it. When they came back out Mrs. MacGuire was with them. After the man left, Miss Elson said, "He might have been my brother, he looked so much like him."

"The one who was torpedoed at the beginning of the war?"

"He's the only brother I had." Her face slid back to its usual determined expression. "That's a closed book now."

A sudden thought struck me. That man looked sort of like Malcolm: same sandy hair, same brilliant blue eyes, same quick way of walking, same sudden smile. I bet Malcolm reminds her of her brother, too. Miss Elson is part of a family! It was confusing: everybody was fond of Malcolm; nobody liked Miss Elson. Maybe that's how it had been when she was a kid with her brother. I wondered.

13

A couple of weeks later we stood in line at the train station, waiting once again to be put somewhere; but so were mobs of people from Calcutta. Many of them had been sleeping on the stone pavement to hold their places near the train, or maybe that's where they had to sleep every night.

"Buy my bananas! Good, cheap bananas!" a man with a tray on his head yelled.

"Buy my jalabees! Fresh-fried jalabees!"

"Baksheesh! Baksheesh!" two little boys called, holding out cupped hands.

A coolie with sweat rolling down his face pushed a cart piled higher than himself. We squashed back.

The train steamed and snorted, scattering cinders on our heads and noses.

Every now and then Mr. Kingsley made some excited remark about "the glory of the British Empire." Over the racket we heard bits about "that booking office now, a monument to the durability of British construction." He probably saw it all clearly: he was tall enough; but through gaps in the crowds we merely glimpsed the English signs, pillars, and arches. In a final burst of enthusiasm he told us, "Calcutta was founded by the British!"

But most of my attention was taken with trying to hang on to Simeon. He'd never seen a train before and wriggled his way through the crowd to look at the engine and the trainmen with their wrenches and oilcans.

I hollered, "Simeon, don't go off like that!" I reached past a turbaned Sikh and grabbed his wrist.

"I even saw a man turning a nut with his wrench. Boy, do I wish I could be a trainman." He bumped past the Sikh, hardly noticing the robes brushing across his face.

I held his wrist tighter. "Don't go off again! You'll get lost!"

He looked at me with candle-bright eyes. "I even saw the engineer. Wouldn't it be jolly to drive a train all your life." He gave a long, glad sigh and stared at the smokestack, which we could just see above the heads of the crowd, as though the only sounds in his ears were train steam and train whistles. I gave up scolding.

After a while I turned to Anne and let go of Simeon's hand, to point hurriedly at a mother sitting against a post with twin babies asleep in her lap. When I reached for Simeon he wasn't there. Why does he act so crazy around engines, I wondered irritably, and stood on tiptoe, but it didn't help at all. A very fat man smelling strongly of curry pushed past us, almost knocking us over.

"You're lucky you don't have a brother you gotta watch," I grumbled to Anne.

"Sometimes, I guess."

"All the time, I know."

"Don't be such a duffer."

"You dope!" I hollered at Simeon as he squirmed between two sweaty men. But it wasn't Simeon.

A man shouted something through a dark red megaphone.

"Time to get on. Follow me," Mr. Kingsley called, and pushed toward the train. We struggled after him through the crowds. Simeon was nowhere.

Very slowly the train began to roll out of the station. There was some sort of mixup with our arrangements. Mr. Kingsley left us and zigzagged his way with surprising speed down the platform toward the engine, bellowing and shaking both hands over his head.

As the fifth carriage slid past us, I saw Simeon and Malcolm waving frantically behind one of the windows. Even Malcolm looked scared.

"Simeon! Simeon!" I yelled.

"Stop the train!"

"They're going away! They'll be lost!"

"Stop the train!"

"Mr. Kingsley, get him!"

But the train continued rolling past, appearing and disappearing through the steam. Passengers still scrambled into the carriages or onto the roof. The eighth carriage. The ninth carriage. The tenth carriage. The whistle shrieked, steam billowed. The train halted.

"It won't move. Get on now," Mr. Kingsley shouted over the bedlam. We squirmed into the space made for us by the crowd.

The benches on the train faced each other in two long rows, but you couldn't see anyone on the other side: there were so many passengers standing squashed in the middle, swaying now with the motion. Simeon sat sobbing on one side of me and Anne sat on the other. It was so hot we stuck to each other and to the wooden slats of the benches.

"I still don't understand how you ever got on the train."

"Malcolm," Simeon sobbed. "Malcolm said it was the right train. I might as well get on with him."

"Well, if you'd stayed with me, it wouldn't have happened. Holding my hand, I mean. He doesn't know everything."

The train slung around a curve, throwing us into a tight pile. As it clicked and steamed onto a straight section of track, we unstuck ourselves and sat up again.

"How long do we have to stay here?" Simeon hiccupped.

"Here in India?" I asked.

"Mmm."

"Till the war's over, I guess."

"How far is where we're going from Mummy and Daddy?"

"I dunno."

"When'll we see them again?"

"You dummy, how'm I supposed to know." He gave me a hopeless look and started biting his nails. "If you keep doing that, you won't have any nails left at all."

"How did you two get together?" Miss Elson's voice chopped down.

Anne and I shrugged.

"That's no way to answer." She took Anne by the

shoulder and pushed her to a new place down the row. "That should keep you out of trouble," she told us, and lurched on down the carriage, checking the others.

Anne gave Miss Elson's back a what's-the-matter-with-you look, then flopped back in her place. Her red curls stood out every which way in the damp heat. Beads of perspiration glinted across her forehead. Her round cheeks were even rosier than usual: cross, thoroughly cross.

I wormed back in my seat. I was really mad. I hadn't done even one bad thing that day, but Miss Elson sure made me want to. My eyes shot pins into her. Simeon patted my hand; he always hated to see me scolded, but I turned on him and hissed, "Leave me alone, you dope." He wilted beside me.

We batted at the teasing little flies which buzzed in our sweaty faces, climbed on our sticky arms, and tangled in our hair. I got tired of flailing at them. My neck was sore from looking up. I was tired of looking at the middles of people, and tired of trying to look out the window behind us.

Mile after mile Simeon went on sitting without moving, without so much as looking up; even when people left and the train got emptier, he didn't look up. Irritably I thought, I wish he'd do something.

Then, for some quirky reason I pushed Simeon. He wasn't expecting it. He lurched off the bench, hit his head on the iron bench leg, and started bleeding. I froze, shut my eyes, and braced myself for the reprimand.

"What happened?" a gentle voice asked.

My eyes snapped open. It was Mrs. MacGuire

and she held Simeon in her lap. She patted him and wiped his head with her hanky.

He said nothing, but leaned his face against her shoulder and cried soundlessly. I shrank into a measly, dried-up worm, and all the madness shrank with me while I stared at my little brother's back.

Mrs. MacGuire put him back on the seat.

"Simeon, do you want to sleep here?" I asked, patting my lap. He gave a happy sigh, put his head down, and was asleep in no time.

The joggling, the *clickety-clickety* of the tracks, and the heat made us all drowsy. Everyone dozed, even the few people left standing in the middle, even the flies.

The train clanked to a stop. "Are we there?" Simeon asked from my lap.

"No, but it's getting dark."

"Are we going all night?"

"I guess so."

We sort of slept, waking enough at little stations to notice more waiting crowds. At the last one I joggled Simeon's shoulder. "We're not there, Simeon, but we gotta get off."

Stupid with fatigue we stumbled off the train and onto a dirt strip by the track. "That train? We're getting on that train now?" I blinked, shook my head, and pointed in the slanting morning light at a tiny train on a parallel track. "Is it real?"

"One, two, three, four, five, six, and the engine." Simeon nodded at each small carriage, thoroughly awake. "Of course it's real. Look. The engine's steaming and people are getting on."

An Indian boy watched us, grinning at our surprise. "It is real. It is called the Toy Train because it is that small." He waved to us, picked up his cloth bundle, and trotted off down the tracks.

The little train had a carnival air to it and jerked briskly forward. Alternately we squinted against the sun, then looked out over the mountains as the train zigzagged east, then west, to take the slopes of the first range of hills. After a while the light grew dim and green.

"They're tickly," Simeon said. The branches of the dense green jungle grew right up to the track and brushed across his outstretched hands.

The train chugged more slowly at each sharp bend, then dashed ahead to the next one, always upward and northward.

"Mr. Kingsley, what are those?" I asked. "There are so many all the same." I pointed at the thousands of glossy-leaved bushes stretching away on each side, growing on terraces which climbed the steep mountains in every direction.

"Tea plantations. In a while we'll be at Mt. Darjeeling, where some of the most famous tea in the world is grown."

"Is this train going right to the top of all these mountains?" Simeon asked.

Mr. Kingsley smiled. "These are just the hills, Simeon, the foothills of the highest mountains in the world. We're at about five thousand feet now. No train goes to the top."

"I thought Mt. Everest was the highest in the world," Anne said. The light grew dim again as the train rounded another mountain and climbed through a fragrant pine forest.

"It is and Kalimpong is only about one hundred miles from it."

"Is that the name of where we're going? Does the train go right to our new school?" Simeon asked eagerly.

"No, first a truck, then a bit of a walk."

We reached Kalimpong, where we were loaded into a couple of trucks, which groaned and rattled up a steep, winding road. After a time the road narrowed and we walked behind the line of coolies who carried our luggage along the footpath.

We paused near a poinsettia grove. "Do you hear singing?" I asked.

"Yes, I hear singing. I wonder who is singing," Anne almost chanted.

"Maybe angels are singing."

"Beautiful, beautiful singing. Over there!" She pointed up the road, a little to the left, to where a church stood, glowing in the evening light. We ran to the open door and peered in. There were hundreds of children, with golden brown faces, all dressed in blue, hundreds of children singing Evensong.

The path wound past several large white cottages with flower gardens in front.

"Who are all those kids?" we asked Mr. Kingsley.

"Children," he corrected absently. "They're Anglo-Indian orphans, most of them, or they've been abandoned."

"Abandoned!" I echoed in disbelief, thinking of the boy who'd been near the door and given us a friendly grin.

The path curved into a small isolated valley and

stopped at an empty cottage. "It looks kind of small for our school," I said doubtfully.

Mr. Kingsley pointed down the steep hill. "Classes will be down there. You can barely see the roof."

The cottage was pleasant and airy, with a wide verandah running all around it. Everything was clean; not even one fingerprint marked the freshly whitewashed walls. In front of the cottage a garden of flowers blew to and fro in the breeze: pink and crimson saucers, blue and purple spires.

"Will we live here?" Simeon asked.

"Yes, that's what they said," I answered.

"For a few years, do you think?"

"I don't know how long. Maybe a few years."

"For a few months, perhaps?"

"I don't know. Maybe."

Simeon's voice grew very eager, almost a whisper. "For a few weeks? Do you think just a few weeks and we can go home?"

"I don't know how long. Until the war ends, anyway. Maybe just a few weeks. I just don't know."

14

"Cops and robbers. Who's for Cops and robbers," Malcolm hollered. Four or five stars were out: the perfect time for the game. From inside the cottage, from behind the laundry shed, from the hedges, kids ran toward Malcolm.

I dashed over. Simeon stood marooned on the verandah, leaning forlornly against a post while Paul waited below him on the grass. "Come on, you two," I shouted as I dashed by.

"He says he doesn't really want to," Paul yelled, jerking his thumb at Simeon.

I stopped and came back. "How come?"

Simeon shrugged and turned away.

"Come on. There's nothing else for you to do. Everyone's playing," I said. He let us drag him along. "You're usually robbers. Why don't you get a head start. I'll watch."

Simeon sighed, then started up the steeply terraced hillside behind the cottage. Paul followed, herding him toward a scattering of bushes.

It was three weeks since we had arrived. Simeon was waiting for a letter from home, but none came. In the afternoons he sat slumped on the verandah. I suppose part of the trouble was that everything about Kalimpong was so different. There were no safe compound walls, no people to speak of, no comfortable noise of shouting and selling, no quarreling even.

"One . . . ten . . . twenty . . . thirty . . ." the cops yelled.

I crawled along the foot of a terrace which was just a little higher than the middle of my back, then crept behind a tickly little bush which grew next to a rockpile.

"D'you think they've had enough time?" I heard the voice of one cop off to the right, where they'd made their jail.

"Nah, better wait a few more minutes." Silence.

Crickets. Two chipmunks scuttering home. "Okay now. Ready or not, here we come . . . come . . . come . . ." a loud yell echoed eerily over our hill. "Shall we hunt in a group or fan out tonight?" A pause and muttering. "Okay." Twigs crackled, pebbles rolled, hard breathing sounded from several directions. I crouched as low as I could. A stone pushed into my back and a branch scratched my neck, but I stayed put. If I moved even a little bit, stones would go bouncing down the hill and betray my place.

Pretty soon I heard the shrieking and laughing of the first person caught, then the distant giggling and stealthy footsteps as that person tried to get free but was caught again and held in the jail.

Footsteps crunched along on the terrace above me. I pressed my face into my knees and held my breath.

Suddenly I heard a shout. Several large stones rolled over the edge of the terrace. Somebody laughed. "Keep jumping, Paul!" Simeon hollered. Underbrush crashed and more stones clattered down as the boys jumped over the terraces higher up the hill.

Then I realized Simeon and Paul were heading right toward me and the rockpile, which you couldn't see properly until you were almost on it. The dusk made it worse. I scrambled up to warn them, but just then Paul came hurtling over the edge with Simeon close behind. Paul shrieked, then started crying hard. "Ow! Ow! Ow! I'm broken to bits! Ow!" Simeon scrambled to his feet from where he'd landed, and I climbed over the rockpile. Paul kept on howling.

"What's the matter? Where are you hurt?" I bent over him.

The cop, who was Malcolm, jumped off the terrace and knelt by Paul. "Here? Does it hurt here?" he asked, gently touching Paul's shoulder, which was pushed forward by a sharp rock.

"No," Paul howled. "Ow! Ow!"

Before long, most of the kids had gathered around and pressed together for a better look. It was hard to see in the dusk.

"What's the matter?"

"I don't know."

"I think he's hurt."

"Of course, goosy, but where?"

Malcolm checked Paul over carefully. "Norman, Go get Mr. Kingsley! Quick as you can!" Malcolm ordered his younger brother. "Tell him Paul's broken his leg!" We all looked down. His left leg had an extra joint below his knee. Blood trickled into his sock. Norman ran.

"I'm broken every place!" Paul wailed.

Two days later, when school was out, Simeon asked Mrs. MacGuire, "Can we go see Paul? In that hospital?"

"You're all going tomorrow morning to give him a surprise. You'll hear tonight."

"And can we see him then? I need to see him. I'm his friend." Simeon stood with his hands in his shorts pockets, looking earnestly up at Mrs. MacGuire.

"Yes. You'll talk to him." She gave him her busy little smile and hustled off.

"Friend hurt?" the floorboy asked.

"Yes. My friend broke his leg."

"Bad thing. Break leg. Lots hurt," the floorboy answered, looking very worried. He was more like a genial cousin than a servant, and his work looked like a game. He seemed to spend all day gliding up and down those glossy floors with waxing pads strapped to his bare brown feet. The pink soles of his feet showed each time he took a step. When we asked to do it, he just winked. He knew that we knew the rules. Simeon and Paul were especially fond of him and often sat in the doorway watching him and chatting. "Tell friend I sad," he said, and glided on down the hall.

"Mail call!" sounded from the verandah.

In a while Simeon stuck his head out the door and glumly watched Mr. Kingsley.

"Come on, Simeon," I shouted. "We've got one." It looked like badly cut paper lace, with sentences which the censors thought might possibly be useful to the enemy trimmed out. We knelt on the verandah and spread our two letters to try to make sense of them.

"You read mine, Ruth," Simeon said irritably. "There's too many holes."

" 'Soon Mummy is expecting a . . .' " Then there was a long hole. " '. . . because the bolt you helped me with on my bike is broken again . . .' "

"What's Mummy expecting?"

"I don't know. There's a hole."

"My dad says the German people are killing Jews, lots of them," Anne announced.

"They can't kill Jews. They're in the Bible," Simeon said without even glancing up.

"Yes, they can. They're real and alive and they live in Germany, except they're being killed."

"Real Jews?" Simeon asked incredulously. "You mean you can talk to a real alive Jew if you want? One of God's people?"

"Yep."

"You're not fibbing?"

"No."

"And those Germans are really killing God's people?"

"Yep." Anne nodded and pointed to her letter.

"How do they dare to kill God's people," Simeon muttered. "The wrath of God will be upon them." He frowned and shook his head like our father. "It must be that Hitler man making them kill. Boy, am I glad I'm not in Germany."

The bell rang. We folded our letters as best we could and stuffed them back in the envelopes.

Before the sun rose next morning, while the sky was still gray and uncertain and the dirt path was still damp from the night, we got up and followed Mr. Kingsley in a sleepy crocodile.

"Come and sit down here," Mr. Kingsley said when we got near the hospital. "Watch carefully."

"What are we supposed to watch, Anne?" I asked, stupidly staring across the valley.

"The sunrise, silly."

We waited, half asleep. A couple of kids put their faces on their knees and dozed.

"Ruth!" Anne poked me awake.

A bird chirped doubtfully. Several more answered. A choir of birds burst into chattering and singing, as slowly, mysteriously, the light began to change. Gradually the trees turned green, the dull snow mountains turned a little bit pink, then almost red, and finally golden as the roof of a rich temple.

We let go of our breath in a hugely satisfied sigh.

"As quietly as you can now." Mr. Kingsley motioned for us to follow. "That's the window. Right at the corner." He pointed toward the little hospital.

Simeon scrambled to his feet and ran, waiting for nobody. He leaned one hand on the brick wall and tried to touch the window ledge, but he was too short. "He's in there! Paul's in there!"

Anne chuckled. "He'd climb right in if he could."

"Ready? Mmmm," Mr. Kingsley hummed the first note of the round we had learned to sing as a morning surprise for Paul. The tune was "Are you sleeping, Brother John?"

> Kanchenjunga, Kanchenjunga,
> Makalu, Makalu,
> Everest and Kamet,
> Everest and Kamet:
> all in view, all in view.

"Sing it once more," an Indian said as she opened the window wide. She wore a white sari with a scarlet border. "Sing it once more," she said in careful English.

"My friend is in there!" Simeon stood on tiptoe and reached up. She leaned down and patted his hand, then disappeared briefly. Just as we began again to sing, she pushed Paul's bed right next to the window.

"That was a good surprise," Paul said, and waved.

"Are you better yet? Can you come back to school yet?" Simeon asked.

"We must not let him be cold," the nurse said, smiling and pulling the window closed. "I will get you because you are the friend," she told Simeon. In a few minutes she reappeared. "Come."

Simeon flushed with pleasure and took her hand. She lifted his hand and looked at the back of it. "You have had a bad injury also."

"It's much bigger than that." Simeon yanked off his sweater, pulled up his shirt sleeve, and showed the scar which stretched almost to his shoulder. "Our cow at home did it," he proudly told her. "With its horn."

"That was terrible!" Lightly she ran her fingers down the scar. "I am happy you are well now."

When he came back out Simeon told us, "Paul has to stay a week, but I'm allowed to visit him."

He found smooth stones, odd-shaped sticks, and strange seedpods to take to Paul.

One day I went with him. "Look what she gave me!" Paul said. He opened the cover of his Bible and showed us the nurse's photograph pasted opposite the one of his parents.

"You like her that much!" I gasped.

He nodded happily. "And you know what she said?"

We shook our heads.

"She said soon the monsoon season's coming."

"What's that?"

"It rains all the time—one hundred and twenty inches in ninety days."

"That's stupid," I said. "I'm almost forty-eight inches. It'd have to rain hard every day for weeks and weeks."

15

Monica stood herself beside me on the verandah with spool and nail, and began expertly to do her French knitting. Every ten rows of yellow she put in one of brown. The tail jerked every time she held it up to count the brown rings. "Mine's longer than anybody's," she gloated. "It's getting near my middle." She held it against herself to show us. Her little eyes glinted through her glasses.

"Who cares!"

"Look at that pride bump swelling!"

"Oh, go jump in the rain gully!"

All June the monsoon rains poured down, sheeting off the roof of the verandah, which was the only place to play. The French knitting craze hit almost everyone, and went on so long we began to measure time by the length of our work.

"Here's the day you slipped and got mud all over your chair at school," Monica told Anne. "And here's the day Faith almost fell in the gully and would've got drowned, except I came along." She held up her tail, pinched between thumb and forefinger at the correct brown ring, then sat down.

"No," I argued. "It was here." I laid my knitting across her lap for her to check the spot.

"I know exactly when it happened," Monica said smugly. She whisked her work across the verandah in front of us, brushed mine off her lap, and knelt to count out her brown rings all over again.

Five or six other kids leaned forward from the wall to see what the argument was about.

"Remember when Paul got his cast off? It was after the rain began, at this stitch, because it got twisted that day and I didn't change it," Anne said. She held up her tail, swished it back and forth a few times, and pointed to a particularly loose, twisted stitch which stuck out from her lumpy maroon knitting, several inches below her spool.

"Wasn't it here?" I questioned. "Because my green was just beginning to come through and that was before you made that stitch."

"I know. I'm watching." Monica's mouth set in a short, straight line like a slot for a penny. "It was here!"

"I know where your box of earwigs is. I've seen them," I taunted, irritated by her constant smugness. "What're they for, anyway?"

"They're my pets."

"Ugh! What horrible pets."

"They're a nice color at least," Anne's comfortable voice broke in. "Kind of like the brown in your knitting. Look at me. Another mistake." She wagged her knobbly knitting in front of us and chuckled. As usual she had stopped an argument without even thinking what she was doing.

The day Monica's knitting reached from her middle to the ground, the letter came. The first part was ordinary enough. "What does yours say?" I asked Simeon.

We were crouched on the verandah with about twenty other kids hunched here and there. Simeon's page was spread out in front of him, and the verandah showed through the censor holes. " 'Hongen-does-not-like-to-study,' " he read, pointing at each word.

"Mine says Aunt Ruth has a Victory Garden."

"What's a Victory Garden?"

"They grow vegetables to win the war."

"Carrots and cabbages marching down the street to win the war?" Averell teased.

"No. Soldiers marching down the street eating the carrots and cabbages."

"Why do carrots and cabbages make them win wars?" Simeon asked.

"Cabbages make them healthy, I guess, and carrots make them see better."

"Oh. 'And-we-have-a-new-baby-brother-called-Ben-ja-min.' " He pronounced it like three Chinese words. "A new baby? Does yours say that?" he asked, as though he didn't believe it.

I looked along the words of my letter. Sure enough, there it was '. . . new baby Benjamin. Here's a bit of his hair. He . . .' Glued to the page was a wisp of almost-white hair. Then there was a big hole, and at the end of it the awful words 'lolling tongue, and big sharp teeth.' That baby must be a monster, I thought, an albino monster because of its white hair. I read some more words, but it was just about some field. Benjamin was a monster-child instead of a sweet little baby brother. Our parents must be telling me about it, but not Simeon, because I was the big sister. Did they want me to get him used to the idea, I wondered.

I looked at Simeon crouched over his letter with his finger on the words "new baby." I slid my letter nearer the edge of the verandah so rain could splash on it and smear the awful words.

"Does it? Does your letter say about a baby?"

"Listen to this," Paul shouted. "A few letters got sneaked out of Weihsien. The kids were all squashed in a temple, but now they're in a bigger concentration camp with lots more people who aren't missionaries."

Simeon poked my arm. "Does it? Does your letter say about a baby?"

"Yes. It's name is Benjamin, but the rain messed part of it."

"Benjamin. Is that how you say it? That's a nice name. I guess . . ." He didn't finish. It was time to put on our raincoats to go down the hill to school. Absently he folded his letter and stuffed it in his pocket as though it were his handkerchief, then he bumped into Paul and started putting on the wrong raincoat; they were both new and lime-green, but Paul's was longer. Clearly the new-baby idea bothered him.

That night I lay in bed, holding my doll and listening to the tiresome rain banging on the iron roof.

Benjamin. I knew that story: his older brother disappeared and Benjamin took his place, which made him the precious son. Would this new baby take our places now? I didn't want to ask the teachers: they wouldn't understand. Nor did I want to write home: the teachers read our letters so the spelling would be right and so we wouldn't tell invented stories.

I couldn't possibly tell Simeon. He didn't have my bounce, as our mother had said. Suddenly I felt as if I had no bounce either. I wanted to cry out loud. I grabbed my doll tight with both hands and pressed her hard against my mouth, so hard it hurt, and cried hot, angry, silent tears: I was tired of being a big sister, tired of the war. It was nearly a year since we had seen our mother and father and I wanted to go home.

When Monica's knitting reached from her shoulder to the ground, it was my week to carry the mid-morning snack down the hill. The tray was neatly piled with sandwiches cut in half and covered with an oilcloth so the rain couldn't get at them, but every day I forgot and the floorboy had to be sent. He'd grin at me and shake his head as he passed the open classroom door. Every noon I was strapped to help me remember for the next day.

Finally, on the fifth day, I remembered. I walked with my bottom lip tight between my teeth, my head at an angle, so I could watch the path underneath the tray. I put my feet down very carefully, curling my bare toes over the edges of the rocks, so as not to slip and dump the whole thing. About halfway down the hill I stopped on the large flat rock, glittery in the rain, and carefully lowered the tray to rest it for a minute against my legs. All the way down the hill yellow, green, and blue raincoats slipped and slid to school.

Automatically I looked off to the right, where a gully ran parallel to the path. It was too wide to jump across and much deeper than our heads when it was dry. But the monsoon had filled it to almost over-flowing with swift, muddy rainwater.

No! I thought. No, they can't be! I shook my head like a dog to get the wet out of my eyes. The tray jiggled. I steadied it. Two lime-green raincoats were wandering farther and farther from the path.

"The dopes! The silly, silly dopes," I muttered. "Come back!" I screeched. "It's dangerous! It's slip-pery! Come back!"

No answer.

"Simeon! Paul! Come back!"

No answer. Of course not. They couldn't hear over the roar of the rain. I started toward them to grab them back. The tray tilted. Quickly I leveled it. The silly daydreamers, I thought, haven't they even a bit of sense in their two heads?

I started running. By now they were about a table length from the gully. My foot slipped. The tray jerked out of my hands. The sandwiches went flying: three sandwiches hit Simeon's bare legs and several more hit Paul's. The two of them stopped, looked down, and slowly turned around. For a few seconds they stared at me lying on my tummy in the rain, reaching toward the empty tray, surrounded by soggy sandwiches.

"Shall we help you pick them up?" Paul asked.

"You silly blokes. Why'd you go to the gully?"
I was mad. I got up.

Simeon's eyes opened very wide. Rain dripped off
his eyelashes. "We were just looking."

"You know it's dangerous. And now look what
happened." I pointed at the sandwiches, which were
scattered all over, blotting up the water.

By now most of the raincoats had disappeared into
the schoolhouse.

"We'll help you pick them up."

"What's the use of that? Who'd want to eat those
things? And it's the first time I remembered."
Simeon and Paul bent over and began scooping up
the horrid things and dumping them on the tray
while I watched. The tray began to fill with rain as
they dumped the sandwiches in. Suddenly I laughed.
Those sandwiches sure looked awful—even a hungry
pig might wonder about them.

"Maybe if Mr. Kingsley sees the sandwiches he'll
know you remembered and you won't get the strap,"
Simeon suggested.

"Good idea." I bent over, too. When we'd collected them all, we covered them with the oilcloth
again, but I don't know why: it sure didn't do them
any good.

"Look at my hands!"

"Hold them out, dummy." I stuck out my hands,
but the rain wouldn't wash away peanut butter. We
cleaned off on the grass.

Mr. Kingsley looked under the oilcloth. "They
don't look too appetizing, do they?" He stared at the
brown heap of sandwiches, squashed and dented by
our fingers. The rain dripped off the hood of my

raincoat and trickled on the edge of the tray. Several kids craned their necks to try and see. "But you did remember them this time." He sighed as though he was tired of me and the whole sandwich business. Then he gave me the surprise of my life: he laughed, a kind amused laugh. "You'll just have to see if you can remember tomorrow, Ruth."

"But tomorrow's Sunday, sir."

He sighed again and I turned toward the hall.

Paul and Simeon were watching anxiously from the door. Simeon jiggled from foot to foot. "Maybe the war will stop soon; and at home you won't have to remember those sandwiches," he whispered, as we hung up our raincoats.

I sighed.

16

But almost a year passed, and as far as we could tell, not very much had changed in the war. We hoped they would soon run out of bombs and soldiers.

One day, at the end of Sunday lunch, Miss Elson laid down her fork and stood up. All chattering stopped. She looked around the dining room, eyeing the laggards in such a way they knew they'd better hustle. "All out for treatment," she said. Everybody had trachoma, a very infectious eye disease. We scowled, filed out to the verandah, and sat along the edge to wait. We looked like a school army. Everyone had grown so much, two sewing women had come to make dresses for the girls, and shirts and shorts for the boys, all the same; like a green girl army and a brown boy army. Miss Elson marched out after us; carrying two pans, one of blue copper sulphate crystals, one of pieces of cotton batting; she stopped at the end of the line nearest the steps.

In a few minutes Mrs. MacGuire came out with a pencil. "Sit straight," she said gently. We craned forward, gritting our teeth as she bent over Monica and expertly flipped her eyelid inside out over the pencil. Miss Elson's arm held the basin of copper sulphate next to Monica's face. Mrs. MacGuire took one crystal, rubbed it several times over the inverted eyelid, then neatly flipped the lid shut, gently pressing the eye closed. She repeated the treatment for Monica's other eye. The whole line flinched and shuddered. Monica barely moved: you had to hand it to her—she got everybody's goat, but when it came to performing for a teacher, she sure was plucky.

When Mrs. MacGuire got to Simeon, he slouched back, making it awkward for her to reach him. Tears stood in his eyes. She waited for him to straighten, but he couldn't bring himself to do it.

"Sit up, Simeon," Miss Elson commanded. "It's a small price to pay for not going blind." Simeon swallowed hard, sucked through his teeth, then sat up slowly. As she continued down the line Miss Elson went on talking in a voice loud enough for everyone to hear. "You are very fortunate children to live here." Automatically she held out the basin of bluestone. "The poor English children . . ." She handed a piece of cotton to Averell, whose eyes were streaming. "Many of them are still in London suffering and dying in the bombing." We knew we were fortunate, but it didn't ease the intense stinging. "You ought to be thankful," she said accusingly. The two teachers left us to think about our blessings. For a couple of hours we just sat, eyes closed, scarcely talking, waiting for the blue miseries to pass.

But there was one reprieve: when the teachers left, the floorboy came down the line with a tray of pink sugar mice, one for each of us. We ate them a nibble at a time, trying to make them last all afternoon.

"Anne," I whispered when my last bite was gone, "I'm beginning to get an idea. I'll tell you later when nobody can hear." She nodded.

Monday morning was a relief. We trooped down the hill cheerfully, discussing the war.

"I wonder if we're ever going to get home or if we'll have to wait here till the Last Judgment," Paul said.

"You've got the Last Judgment on the brain," Megan complained.

"Not likely," Anne burst out. "That's a terribly long time. It's already 1944, and this war's got to end sometime."

"Not if they don't win or agree or something."

"Oh, they're all sending telegrams to each other."

"Who?"

"King George and Winston Churchill and Generalissimo Chiang Kai-shek and Hitler and Frank . . . Frank . . . Who's that American one, Ruth?"

"Well," Paul said thoughtfully, "whatever they're

doing, maybe they're trying, but the bad ones are still winning."

"Who says! They're shooting and bombing and attacking and whatever else they do. Sometime they'll win," Anne explained.

"Who?"

"Our side. Britons never never shall be slaves, you know."

"Mmm, but that's not the Chinese."

"The Japanese dive-bomb themselves to death. That'll take care of them." She made the motion with her hand.

"Oh." Paul frowned. "That doesn't seem like a very good way to win."

"It isn't, but it's what they do. It's their religion or something."

"I still don't believe you about those Jews," Simeon said.

"Yeah," a couple of other kids sneered. "You're just making it up."

"If my dad says they're real, then they're real," Anne retorted. "Don't you agree, Ruth?"

I frowned at her. I'd been only half listening. The idea that I'd been working on had a few problems. "We could ask Mr. Kingsley," I suggested.

Mr. Kingsley usually kept the class right on the topic, but once in a while he let us ask unrelated questions, usually about the war. Simeon put up his hand. "Anne says there are really alive Jews in Germany and the Germans are killing them. Is that true, Mr. Kingsley?" There was a buzz of interest.

Mr. Kingsley plucked at the stiff gray hair near his

ear. "Yes. The Germans are searching out the Jews to kill them, just as St. Paul before his conversion hunted out the Christians to kill them," he said, trying to get us back to Scripture class, but we wanted to know more.

"Does that mean all the Germans are bad people?"

Mr. Kingsley sighed and his walleye jerked. A strange look came over his face as he slowly closed his Bible, came around to the front of his desk, and sat on the edge. Slowly he rubbed his thumb up and down his beaky nose. You could have heard a paper slide to the floor. "War is like this," he said, and held up a mass of tangled kite string. "When you're in the middle of the war you can't tell where the beginning is or the end. Even the good and the bad are sometimes confused."

"You mean the lines of good soldiers get mixed up with the lines of bad soldiers?"

"No. I mean there are good and bad soldiers on both sides. And the confusion is among all the people. In Germany now, there are German Christians in jail." He put the string back on his desk.

"The Japanese. Are the Japanese all bad?"

"No. I'm sure there are many Japanese for whom this war is a heartache."

"What about the English?"

His voice changed to a more comfortable one. "There are mistaken Englishmen, of course. But the English are an enlightened race."

"What about Americans?"

"Well, um, the Americans." He looked amused and a bit uncomfortable. "They mean well. They're certainly generous with men and materials. But . . . they're rather like children. They've a lot to learn."

"And New Zealanders?" Anne asked. "What about New Zealanders?"

Mr. Kingsley grunted and walked back behind his desk. "It's time to get to class now. Let's see. Where were we?" He opened his Bible and started looking down the page. "Ah yes. Here we are. St. Paul's ship is at the port of Fair Haven."

By the end of school my plan was complete. I wanted desperately to go home to see our new baby, who seemed always to have a cough. Our mother's letters often told about it. Our father's hardly mentioned the baby and that made me suspicious; his letters were about church meetings and sermons. But if I remembered about babies, ours should be standing or maybe stepping by now.

"Come on," I said to Anne. She followed me to a private place we had near the hedge.

"Bang! Bang!" the shouts of the boys' war game sounded from the other side of the verandah, followed by the sound of running feet and an angry scuffle.

Then some girls' voices. "You're out. It's not fair. You're out."

"What d'you want to do?" Anne asked.

I explained my plan.

"But we don't know Nepalese or Hindustani or any of the languages they talk around here," she objected. "And it'd take a donkey's age to learn. Anyhow, what'll we preach about?"

"We'll think about that when we find the right people. And in Calcutta some of the heathen talk English."

"Calcutta! That's too far away. We'd be tired out. Think how long the train trip was!"

"We'll save our food and then we can walk."

"Walk! You're daft!" She flopped on the grass. I picked off leaf after leaf from the privet hedge. The plan wouldn't be any good without her. Then she sat up and gave a comfortable chuckle. "Okay. When do you want to start?"

Megan and Faith sauntered past. "You two sure get in a lot of trouble."

We stuck out our tongues at them and went on with our schemes. "We can go when we've saved enough bread and raisins. It'll be hard to sneak it out from supper, but I know a good place to hide it."

"Who else is going?"

"Hmm. Simeon and Paul, of course. Averell, do you think?"

"Averell would be good. He fits into whatever we want and he's strong. Norman's good at figuring things out."

"Okay."

"How come we have to preach the gospel?" she asked.

"In case anybody asks us. It sounds better than running away. And anyhow, it might be a good idea," I explained.

It took quite a while to save enough food to fill our Klim milk box, which we kept in the dark hole under the stairs.

One evening Paul came out of supper with a damp smudge on each side of his shorts. I hissed into his ear, "You shouldn't take out wet food."

"It's not for the trip exactly." He looked uneasy.

"Show me."

He stuck his hands in his pockets and pulled out several soggy lumps. "I don't like it. I'm going to throw it away."

"Better chuck it now while nobody's looking. And you better wash your hands. You smell funny."

On his hands lay several soggy bits of partly chewed liver. I could hardly blame him for not liking the stuff: nobody did; nobody had thought of his way of getting rid of it, either.

"You won't tell?"

"Course not. I think it's a good idea except for the smudges where your pockets are."

Simeon came over to see what was going on. "Are we really going back home to Daddy and Mummy when we've got to Calcutta?"

"Yep. But first we have to preach the gospel to the heathen and give them this money." I showed him some copper annas we had found.

"Is anyone else coming?"

"Yep."

"How?"

"How what?"

"How'll we all get home? How'll we get on an airplane?"

"I don't know. We'll see when we get there. Maybe there'll be a nice American soldier someplace."

Simeon held out a sticky pink ball with some bits

of lint stuck to it, all that was left of his sugar mouse. "It's for the box."

"You don't have to put something special like that in the box."

He popped it in his mouth, then said, "You know what Monica says?" I shook my head. "She said Miss Elson gets them for us."

I laughed. "Monica sure thinks up some whoppers."

"She says it's really true," Simeon insisted.

"Well, get her to show us. I think it's a big fat whopper."

But on Sunday, when Monica's eyes had been treated and she was taking the cotton from Miss Elson, she said, "Thank you for the sugar mice."

Miss Elson said, "The cook makes them," and moved abruptly to the next child.

"But I heard . . ." Monica began.

"You know you order them for the children, Florence," Mrs. MacGuire chided.

Miss Elson looked icily at her and said nothing.

17

After lunch, on the third Saturday of our plan, we escaped. We masqueraded our way up the steep hill behind the school as though playing a game of sardines: one person faced the school, counting loudly, but actually keeping watch.

"... nine, ten ..." Norman bellowed until the hills echoed.

"I didn't mean *that* loud," Anne hissed. "Somebody'll want to come play with us." She grabbed Paul's wrist and I grabbed Simeon's, dragging them up as fast as we could to the next patch of bushes. Averell squeezed in with the box.

The mock-game zigzagged higher and higher. Simeon kept glancing back over his right shoulder, giving scared little sniffs. When we reached the top we paused a moment to look down at the cottage, a dollhouse from this height.

"Look at those blokes. They don't even know we're gone!" Anne gloated.

"Let's get over the top quick," Simeon whispered. We raced over the crest of the hill and onto the main mountain path from Tibet to Darjeeling. Simeon heaved a big glad sigh of relief and began to enjoy himself. "Look how far down it is!" He pointed to a silver path which was a river far away at the foot of the mountain. By now we were farther than we'd ever been, escaped from school, free!

The path to Darjeeling was cut into the side of the mountain, which sloped very steeply down to the river. On the other side of the river, behind the first green range, rose the gigantic Himalayan snow mountains, and behind those mountains there was nothing but blue sky.

We walked along the gravelly path, occasionally chucking stones for the sheer joy of it. They never rolled very far because of all the bushes. The sun slid down the sky.

"What'll we do if it's night?" Simeon asked suddenly.

Anne flopped down at the side of the path, her face flushed. "I'm tired."

"Lazybones," Averell teased.

"Yep, I'm a lazybones," she said amiably. "Look!" She pointed along the path. "I see some travelers coming."

"Who's got the money?" Simeon whispered excitedly.

"Here." Averell fished it out of his pocket. We all crowded into the bushes at one side since the path wasn't any too wide. Averell put the money on four flat stones in a row across the path, and then we waited.

There were four men, not as tall as Mr. Kingsley and much stockier. Three of them wore dark blue robes and one a dark brown one, all rather patched and faded. Their robes were tucked into their belts to make bulgy carrying bags for whatever they needed with them, mostly food, I guess, and maybe knives. As they got closer we could see that their faces looked familiarly Chinese rather than Indian. When they reached us, we pointed and nodded and smiled. The travelers did the same, picked up the money, and walked swiftly down the path. We burst out of the bushes.

"It worked! It worked!" I said, twirling round on my toes. "It's not exactly preaching the gospel, but it's giving unto others."

"I liked their faces," Norman said dreamily. "They looked Chinese."

Simeon sang, "Sailing home, sailing home." The hymn writer meant to heaven, but Simeon meant home to our mother and father. Our plan was working beautifully.

Norman looked thoughtfully up the path. "I wonder if Tibetans are really Chinese. Maybe we could go home that way."

"Yep. They are, my dad says." Anne held up her hand to him. "Give us a pull." Absently, Norman reached down and yanked Anne to her feet.

We passed several groves of poinsettias which grew a good bit higher than our heads. Their flowers were such a brilliant red they looked like a New Year celebration for us.

"My legs are getting tired. How many more miles to Calcutta?" Simeon asked after a while.

Anne said, "I'm fagged out. Let's have a snack now."

"Piggy!" Averell held the box just out of her reach. Anne chuckled.

We sat down in the middle of the path and opened our Klim milk box. Even though the bread and raisins were dried out, that picnic tasted much better than the fresh food at school in the dining room.

Paul stood up, reached to the bottom of his pocket, and pulled out his glass snowstorm.

"What've you got?" Averell asked.

Paul shook the globe and held it up, smiling a little as the snow swirled around the little boy and slowly settled.

"Do it again."

We watched for maybe ten minutes.

"The rest of the food's for later." I stood up, closed the box, and looked for a stream to take the dryness out of our mouths. Before we'd gone very far, we were tangled in a patch of bramble bushes.

"Stop! All of you. Stop!" The command slammed across the valley. Our stomachs went as hollow as soccer balls.

"Who is it?" Simeon whispered behind his hand.

Nobody answered.

Norman squinted toward the sound. "It's my brother," he said in disgust. "It would be."

"Wait! Wait right where you are." Malcolm and Keith, the two biggest boys in our school, stood on the ridge above us. "Wait!" they yelled again, and scrambled toward where we stood, planted in the path.

Simeon's frown deepened as he watched them. "Do they mean we can't go?"

Averell nodded.

"If you come right now," Malcolm panted at us, "only the leader will get the strap." He looked at everybody except Anne and me. Sweat dripped off the end of his stubby nose. His face was almost as red as the poinsettias, but angry. He puffed a bit more. "But if you make any trouble, you'll all get a strapping you'll never forget. Mr. Kingsley is back there." He pointed up the ridge.

Nobody moved.

Malcolm stepped toward his brother as if to grab him, but still we didn't move. Everyone looked sick. Finally Averell and Paul took two draggy steps and we all followed like prisoners.

The golden afternoon sun gleamed on the polished floorboards of the hall where we were told to line up against the wall. Half a dozen boys passed the doorway and stared curiously. The floorboy walked smartly past, carrying an armload of folded sheets. As always he smiled at us.

"Simeon, you went, too?" Mrs. MacGuire said sorrowfully.

"It wasn't Simeon's fault!" I almost yelled. "I told him to. I thought we'd be able to get back to China after we'd preached the gospel to the heathen in Calcutta." The words flew out of my mouth. Miss Elson came by and stopped to listen, though I scarcely noticed.

Mrs. MacGuire blinked and looked back and forth along the line. Then she said, "After you'd—"

"Preached the gospel to the heathen," I said again, and explained all our careful plans. Mrs. MacGuire had no more words for us, no more words of any kind; but she didn't look angry, just greatly astonished.

"You are learning," Miss Elson said when I'd finished. Her voice was flat, giving no clue to what she had in mind. I looked at her, puzzled, but her face gave me no hint.

Nobody was strapped. We were all sent to bed early without supper, except for what was left of our bread and raisins. I lay thinking of what fun it had been even if it hadn't worked.

The rest of the girls came to bed, but still I wasn't sleepy. Somebody down the line started scratching a mosquito bite. I flipped over on my tummy to look at the sky, growing a deeper and deeper blue, framed by our window. In the upper left-hand corner one star shone by itself. Simeon had looked so small and alone against the doorframe, cowering with fear and hurt and miserable disappointment. But I'd fix that. I pulled my Bible out from under the bed, opened the floppy black cover, and looked at my mother and father. "You wait," I told them. "I'll figure out some way yet."

Suddenly I had a thought. This is the first time I've stuck up for Simeon! The first time I've shouted out it was my fault. Maybe that's what Miss Elson meant when she said I was learning.

18

One morning toward the end of the year, Mr. Kingsley made an announcement after prayers. "Hannah Wurtmueller will be coming today," he said. "It'll be hard for her being the only new child, and you may need to speak a little slowly since she is German."

Everyone jerked to shocked attention. If Mr. Kingsley had said, "She has the face of a lion and four wings and human hands under the wings and her whole body is full of eyes," like Ezekiel's vision, if he had told us all that, we could hardly have been more shocked. An alive German was coming!

All the way down the hill to school we talked about one thing and came to one miserable conclusion:

The new girl was German.

The Germans killed God's people, the Jews, the most special people on earth.

You didn't talk to people who killed God's people.

Therefore, we wouldn't talk to the new girl.

We would send her to Coventry.

It was as simple as that.

That afternoon Mrs. MacGuire stood on the verandah with her arm around the new girl's shoulders. "Come and meet Hannah Wurtmueller," she called. The sunlight was in their eyes so they probably couldn't see us too clearly, which was just as well, since we must have looked like a bunch of sullen refugees.

We waited on the grass below the verandah, and stared up, unsmiling and offended. The new girl was supposed to look different. We had discussed that at recess. "I bet she's fatter than me." Anne held out both hands to indicate tremendous girth.

"I bet she scowls all the time."

"And walks like this." Simeon goose-stepped across the grass, chin tucked in to his chest.

"I bet she has ugly ugly army-green clothes."

"And squinty eyes."

"And warts perhaps? On the end of her nose? Like a witch?" Even Paul was in on the horrible picture we were conjuring up.

But there she stood, a little above us, smiling shyly. She had long dark braids reaching almost to her waist. None of us had long hair, though all the girls wished for it. Every couple of months or so we sat on the edge of the verandah, while either Mrs. MacGuire or Miss Elson worked her way down the line with a pair of sharp scissors, cutting our hair and sometimes snipping the lobes of our ears by accident.

The new girl's clothes were hardly the army-green dreadfuls we'd thought up. Her blouse was white with embroidered flowers around the neck; her skirt was blue and fit her properly. Our clothes were loose and pretty ugly: all cut in a sack shape from a couple of bolts of brown- or green-checked cloth.

When Mrs. MacGuire pushed the new girl forward a little to say something to us, we wanted to hear a gruff voice and really terrible chopped-up English. "I am Hannah," she said. "I hope we can be friends at your school." She spoke with scarcely an accent.

We were outraged.

Then Mrs. MacGuire called Monica, but even Monica could hardly bring herself to obey this time. She looked back over her shoulder at the rest of us and made a questioning face. It's a little hard to keep someone in Coventry when you're supposed to be showing that person around, but she managed somehow.

At night it was easy enough not to say anything. The beds on the right side of the dorm had been pushed down a little to make room for one more in the corner farthest from the door, a little to the left of the third window. We could isolate the new girl in that corner quite easily. We all talked away as we got undressed and folded our clothes, keeping an eye on her but pretending we didn't know she was there. My bed was next to hers, so I had to turn away a bit not to see her. Monica's was right across the aisle, but she always kept to herself anyway, she was in such a hurry to get ready first.

I watched the girl out of the corner of my eye until it gave me a headache. She undressed quickly, folded her clothes very neatly, even her socks; then slid her nightgown over her head, a flowered nightgown with ruffles around the neck and wrists. I sighed enviously. We had plain, boxy pajamas, all alike.

"Hey, someone apple-pied my bed," Faith called out from five beds down.

Megan snickered.

"You! How'd you get up here without getting caught?"

Megan snickered harder and stooped to help Faith straighten her sheet.

Just one more quick look, I thought. The new girl knelt to say her prayers. Before she slid into her covers she pulled out two framed pictures from under her bed and kissed them. Two, I thought, why two?

In the morning Anne asked, "Did you see her eyes? There's for sure something awful about her with eyes like that."

"What about them?"

"One's sort of blue and one's sort of brown. Who ever heard of such funny eyes!"

For six days we continued to ignore her. Hannah went quietly about whatever had to be done, or sat on the verandah steps alone when the rest of us played outside.

One afternoon, during hide-and-seek, I almost

came and grabbed her to hide with me behind the larkspur garden. But I'd have to pass half a dozen kids, and if they saw me with her, they'd hiss.

Late that night I woke up and heard very quiet crying from the bed in the corner. I remembered my first nights at school, that ghastly, empty loneliness. And here was Hannah with everyone cutting her off. Nobody can tell in the dark, I thought; anyhow they're all asleep. Faith snored a little as usual. I reached over to Hannah's bed and squeezed her hand. It was wet. Then we lay quietly, our hands loosely clasped between the two beds.

In the morning Hannah said, "It's hard to be the only new girl. I'm glad you'll be my friend."

I gave her a quick, embarrassed smile and made a careful hospital corner in the sheet of my bed, so that I wouldn't have to look at any of the faces which had suddenly jerked in my direction.

I heard several whispers of "Traitor!"

My cheeks burned.

Hannah looked around, puzzled and hurt, and didn't say any more.

Because Hannah was new and because I was usually naughty, our desks were both at the front of the crowded little classroom. She kept her attention fixed on Mr. Kingsley. That morning when he was writing the thirteen-times table on the blackboard Hannah spoke up without raising her hand. "Mr. Kingsley, sir, the 13 x 8 is 104 not 103."

We were electrified: no kid gave Mr. Kingsley instructions, and Hannah was new. How does she know the thirteen-times table that well, anyway, I wondered. I glanced at her and grinned, greatly admiring her daring. Somebody hissed faintly.

Mr. Kingsley went on standing with his back to us, his left hand with the chalk in it still raised to go on to 13 x 13. "That's correct, Hannah. It was a mistake." He erased the 3 with his thumb and wrote 4.

I sent a note to Anne in the desk just behind mine. "She's German but she's nice. Shall we break Coventry?"

Anne sent back a tiny note folded to the size of my little fingernail. There was one word on it, TRAITOR. Angrily I twisted the paper into a crumb and chucked it into the wastebasket. That dope, I thought. But I didn't talk to Hannah at recess.

When school was over we straggled back up the hill. After the brilliant sunshine outside, the light in the hall was so dim that at first I couldn't see anything. I waited for my eyes to adjust. Hannah sat hunched on the bottom stair twisting her dark braid around and around her finger. Now I was beginning to feel like a traitor, but to Hannah, not to the others. She didn't look up. Impulsively I sat beside her. "D'you want to come play soccer with us?"

Hannah shook her head.

"I guess it does look sort of rough." I sat for a few more minutes, then stood to get a drink. She reached up and touched my hand. "Thank you."

Hannah went off someplace after supper; I was glad. I didn't know how to act with her in front of the others. Anne and I wandered out toward the privet hedge, which had an oddly pleasant smell in the evening. I pinched a few leaves, then put my chin a little in the air. "I broke Coventry today."

"Traitor!"

"I am not. She's really nice and you're a dope if you don't think so."

A funny look came over Anne's face. "Have you seen the pictures under her bed? The ones she kisses at night?"

"No."

"Monica says one of them's Hitler."

"That's stupid!"

"Ask her, then, if you think she's so nice."

"Okay, I will." I crushed a few more privet leaves and sniffed at them, giving myself time to think. "Aren't you getting kind of tired of this Coventry business? Don't you think we've done it long enough?" Anne didn't say anything. I tried again. "Anyhow, even if she's German she's still just another kid."

"She *is* a good sport," Anne said slowly. "I'll say that for her. She hasn't tattled once."

The next day after lunch there was some time before we had to go back to school. "Can I see your pictures? The ones you kiss at night?" I asked Hannah. She smiled, a bit embarrassed, and started up the stairs.

She held out a picture of a man and a woman who reminded me of Mr. and Mrs. Baer. "My father and my mother. I miss them so much."

"What about the other picture?"

A little reluctantly she pulled out the second one.

A man with a mustache stood facing a group of small children, holding out flowers to them. The picture was black and white, with the flowers—I think they were roses—tinted red and yellow. "It is Hitler giving flowers to the little children."

"Hitler! The real wicked Hitler?"

"He's not wicked," she said very earnestly. "He *loves* little children. You're not German so you don't understand. He really loves us, and—"

I was so shocked I walked out.

The third day of the following week I left the strapping room at the end of the dorm and started crossly downstairs. It was my turn for taking sandwiches to school; as usual I forgot and at noon I was strapped. Hannah sat on the bottom step, her head in her lap, crying quietly. Very gruffly I asked, "Why are *you* here? What're *you* crying about?"

"You shouldn't be spanked, just to forget the sandwiches."

"You're crying for that! You're crying for me!"

She nodded.

"But I always forget! I always get spanked!"

"But it is not right."

Miss Elson leaned over the top of the stairs; her pendant clicked against the newel post. "Go along, girls." Her voice was milder than usual. "Don't be late."

We glanced up, grabbed hands, then dashed down the hill, slipping, sliding, and laughing. This time I didn't care who saw me and called me traitor: Hannah was worth being a traitor for.

I dragged her to the pavement where Anne was

drawing a hopscotch diagram. "You know how come she loves Hitler? It's because he loves little children."

Anne looked up from where she was crouched with her piece of soft marking stone and pushed her red curls out of her face with the back of her hand. She didn't say anything, but her face kept changing expression. Finally she smiled. "Want to learn to play hopscotch?"

Hannah nodded. "Yes. I like hopscotch." Anne explained the numbers and where to throw the stone. Hannah must have played it before: she could hop a long time, and could lean down on one foot to pick up the stone without tumbling over. Her braids brushed across the numbers.

For the next few weeks we made a pretty funny trio: Anne and I, who were usually in trouble for one thing or another, and Hannah, who I don't think had ever broken a rule in her life. The others kept all three of us in Coventry, but kids kept forgetting and talking to us. Before long the whole thing was in the past.

19

August 15, 1945. V-J Day.

Evening prayers. Hide-and-seek until dusk. Bedtime. Lights out. All still.

Suddenly Miss Elson stood in the doorway, silhouetted against the glow of the hall lamp. She said,

"Today the war is over." She might have been giving instructions for cleaning up the dorm for all the excitement she put in her voice. We were so foggy with the beginnings of sleep, and there was so little hint of the grandness of the news, that it took a few minutes for us to realize what she had said.

"Anne," I finally whispered, "did you hear? The war is over! Hannah"—I poked her shoulder—"did you hear? We can go home!"

"Is that what she said?"

"Yep."

"The war? Is over?"

"Yep."

"Now we can go home?"

We began to cry with the pure joy of it.

Miss Elson's voice slashed across the semi-darkness. "No crying or you'll be given something to cry for."

I hate her, I thought. I hate her as much as . . . but I couldn't think of anything bad enough. She left.

Monica buried her head under her pillow. Megan's bed squeaked as she got up on her elbow to comfort Faith. Somebody coughed several times.

And then the longing for home washed over me: our mother, our father, our amah, Hongen. I felt a hand on my left arm, Hannah's hand. I held it. Then I felt a hand on my right arm, Anne's hand. I held it. We lay for a minute like that, but it was uncomfortable face down. We all flipped over, giggling very quietly, and again held hands. Anne and Hannah fell asleep.

I got up on bare feet to go to the toilet. Near the end of the hall a wedge of lamplight spilled across the floorboards where Miss Elson's door stood ajar. I walked to the edge of the light and looked in. She sat huddled over a table. Her gray-striped pajamas, her gray hair straggling down her back in mop strings, and her collapsed mouth with no teeth in it made her look useless, like an old refugee left behind.

She was writing a letter with a fountain pen which scratched across the paper. The wooden ring Malcolm had given her clicked faintly as she wrote. Next to the water glass with her teeth in it was something I had to squint to see, until I realized it was her pendant propped open on the heap of chain. It had several parts, like pages in a book. On each of the four inner surfaces was a photograph: two were brownish with age, her parents I suppose; one I couldn't make out, and one was sharply black and white. I squinted harder: it was a man with a military cap. It must have been her brother.

I thought, I guess I can't hate her.

I slept. While I slept I dreamed a very queer dream of censored letters blowing out of the bombers' moon and whirling about. In the midst of the clutter were misty faces with clear eyes: Simeon's and our mother's big brown eyes, and our father's gray eyes. And a face with no eyes. The faces came near me with eyes wide open; then they backed up and faded away with eyes half closed. Sometimes the eyes were glad and welcoming. Sometimes the eyes were stern and disapproving. I awoke and saw that it was a dream, but still I felt muddled and scared.

One afternoon a couple of months later, Anne and I peeked in the teachers' room door, which was slightly ajar. "Hey, Anne," I whispered, "see on that table? It's the passports. Let's look at the pictures."

"Those horrible things?"

We snickered, tiptoed in, and started hunting for our own. Hers was in the middle of the first pile of little books. "You look mad," I told her, pointing at the official black-and-white photograph.

"You're not allowed to smile, so of course I do. I bet yours does, too." She found mine and began giggling as she held it open to me. "You don't even look like you."

"Well, my hair was different, and that was when I first came. I was just a little kid then and—" We heard heavy footsteps on the stairs and ducked out fast.

The next week we left our valley, boarded the train, and bumped over the rails to Calcutta on our way back to China. Simeon said, "I can't wait till we're on a real steamship, can you?" He pushed his soft hair off his face and turned to look at Paul. "Can you?"

Paul had slid down on the train bench so his head came just to the top of the seat and his knees bumped against a smelly old basket of chickens on the floor in front of him. Lazily he rolled his head. "Can I what?"

"Wait till we're on a real steamship."

Paul's knee joggled the basket. The startled chickens squawked excitedly, and several poked their heads out. Some bits of down floated up and made Paul sneeze. Finally he answered, "Mmm. Just think, messing about in boats like Ratty. The ropes. The water. The adventure of it all."

Simeon was indignant. "Not boats, Paul, a steamer. A coastal steamer."

Paul stared at Simeon, smiling dreamily.

Simeon went on, "Wouldn't it be nice if our mothers and fathers were standing on the dock in Shanghai?" One chicken looked inquiringly up at him.

"Hmm?"

"Our mothers and fathers."

"What about them?"

"Wouldn't it be nice if they were on the dock?"

"In Calcutta!"

"No. Shanghai."

Paul said, "They won't. You know that." He sat up with an irritated jerk, knocking against the basket. The chickens flapped and squawked. "Shut up!" he said with unusual sharpness.

20

The dumpy little steamer gave us our first welcome home with her familiar Chinese faces, singsong Chinese talk, and spicy Chinese food. She was a squat cargo ship painted dirty white, with rust stains running down below the deck. Her hull was black with barnacles. Even her name, painted in orange characters over the anchor, had a familiar sound to it, the *Flying Pigeon*.

"What can you see out your portholes?" I shouted to Simeon in the boys' cabin across the hall.

"Nothing. Norman's head's in the way."

"Well, what could you see before it was in the way?"

"Kids. Lots of them swimming in the water waiting for us to throw money, but we haven't got any. What can you see?"

"Lots of brown sacks. There's a thing on the boat hoisting them up."

"Steamer!" he corrected. "Don't you just love to hear Chinese yelling again?"

"I sure do! Good old Chinese coolie-yelling."

The next afternoon the engines throbbed, the shrill steam whistle blew, the horn wailed. Clouds of gritty black smoke poured from the funnel and the whole ship creaked and shuddered. The sea was so rough, all but three or four kids promptly got sick; even the teachers looked green and spent most of those first couple of days lying in their bunks.

But Simeon and Paul felt super. They loved the freedom they had to wander about the ship with no one to tell them where to go or what to do. On the second day Simeon got quite a bruise on his forehead.

"Did you slip?" I asked as he lurched up to our open cabin door.

He looked at Paul and giggled. Soon the two of them were being so silly, clapping their hands over their mouths and doubling with laughter, that I rolled over in my bunk and pulled up my knees, too seasick to bother to find out what they'd been up to.

After supper they came jauntily back down the narrow hall, pretty pleased to still be the only ones well enough to eat that good Chinese food. As Simeon chattered about ropes, winches, and hatches, I noticed he was wearing a funny little black rubber ring on his left middle finger. "What's that thing?" I reached out to touch the glossy rubber.

"A gasket."

"A gasket? What's that?"

"Something so pipes won't leak."

"How'd you get it?"

"A gasket, a gasket, where'd you find a gasket!" he chanted, and swaggered into the boys' cabin.

By the third day most of us had our sea legs and were well enough to start classes. We sat along the edges of the bunks like swallows on a telephone wire. The feet of the kids on the upper bunks barely cleared the heads of those below.

"Simeon," Mr. Kingsley asked, "which country does the Irrawaddy flow through?"

But Simeon was twisting the gasket around his finger while he gazed contentedly at the seagulls swooping past the porthole. "Gasket," he murmured.

"Simeon! Pay attention!" Mr. Kingsley repeated the question. "It's a country you flew over."

"My paper! It flew out the porthole!"

"So's mine. Look!"

"Yes, Anne?" Mr. Kingsley said, darting a glance at the flying papers.

"Assam."

"No. You've got the right journey but the wrong country. The Irrawaddy is in Burma." He held up a small map.

"Show us where we flew. Please, Mr. Kingsley," Anne begged.

He pointed. "Here's Kunming, then here over Burma, then over the Himalayas, the roof of the world, and over . . ."

"Was it dangerous?"

"Very dangerous. They didn't even have proper charts or maps. Many planes crashed flying the 'Hump.' "

We grinned at each other, pleased to have been in such exciting danger.

"What is another major Burmese river?"

"The Salween?" Norman suggested.

"My paper flew out! Look!"

Mr. Kingsley frowned irritably at the paper. "Good, Norman. Look closely. Here it is." Slowly he showed the map around.

After class it was Anne's turn to put away pencils and papers and leave the peculiar classroom tidy. I stayed to help. Then we climbed up the stairs and onto the deck. About half a dozen kids stood in a tight group facing Monica and chanting:

> *Tattletale tit*
> *Your tongue shall be slit*
> *And all the dogs in Kalimpong*
> *Shall have a little bit.*

Monica started crying. Her glasses steamed up. She covered her face with her warty hands and whimpered through her fingers, "Nobody likes me."

The others began again,

> *Nobody loves me.*
> *Everybody hates me.*
> *I'm sitting in the garden*
> *Eating worms.*

She'd given us all little enough reason to like her, but you can't just stand by and watch a kid being harassed by a gang and do nothing.

Anne muttered, "The beasts." We towed Monica down the deck to watch a couple of sailors painting the vents near the ship's bridge. But her gratitude was worse than her smugness. She trailed around after us like a kid fussing along behind a couple of priests, anxious to say something impressive. Finally Anne said, "Do you have something you want to show us, or—"

"You want to see my pet cockroach?" Monica asked happily.

I said, "That's horrible."

"No, it's not."

"Anyhow, you can't have a pet cockroach. It'd scutter off."

"Maybe you can't, but I can." We followed her back down the stairwell to a dark corner of the hallway where a bulletin board hung, covered with Chinese notices and pictures. Over it a dim light with a loose connection flickered like an idol lamp lighting the ancestor scrolls. Monica pointed to the floor. "Look, there he is. That one with the paint." In the corner were several glossy reddish-brown cockroaches. One had a couple of streaks of white paint straggling down its back. All over the steamer were corners with patches of paint so thick that in the salty air they stayed tacky.

"It's dead, I bet."

"No. Look." Monica knelt, took a couple of grains of rice from her pocket, and offered them to the nasty insect. Its antennae waved slowly back and forth as if accepting the gift. It didn't scuttle off the way cockroaches usually do. I think its feet must have been stuck in the paint. Anne and I sighed and went back on deck, leaving Monica alone, crouched before her cockroach.

Halfway down the deck, near the lifeboats, Mr. Kingsley was organizing a group of kids. Simeon broke away from them and dashed over to Anne and me, almost slithering into us along the deck, slippery with salt spray. "Do you want to see the engine room?" he asked in great excitement.

"Sure. When?"

"Right now. Six at a time." We clambered down ladder after ladder, and went through a heavy metal door into a huge room, very noisy with the pounding of the engines. Simeon stuck right beside me. I thought he was scared of the racket, but he didn't put his hands over his ears. There was an enormous shiny metal pole running horizontally the full length of the room and out the back of the steamer. "That's the propeller shaft," he hollered over the noise.

"How'd you know!"

He grinned, enormously pleased with himself. "And see, there's some extra gaskets hanging up."

As we struggled back up and out, I felt more and more puzzled. "How'd you know about that propeller shaft? And those silly gaskets?"

He pushed me away from the others. "Promise not to tell?"

"I promise."

Simeon didn't tell me the whole thing right then, but over the next few days I got the story straight. This is what those boys were up to. The ship was full of doors, some of them firmly latched, some of them firmly hooked back, to prevent any of them from swinging dangerously with the tossing of the steamer. Those first few days Simeon and Paul roamed the steamer peering into the open doors and pressing their ears to the closed doors, like two explorers. They came to one closed door, pressed their ears against the rough white paint, and listened. "Do you hear that?" Simeon whispered.

"Mmm. What is it?"

"I don't know. Shall we open it?"

Together they grabbed the long handle and yanked down on it with all their might and main. It opened with a jerk and hit Simeon's head, bruising it. The two of them peered in. A Chinese man sat on a stool, wearing headphones and a deep frown. With his hand he motioned them to stand quietly inside the door. They grimaced and stepped up over the high metal threshold, which came nearly to their knees, and into the tiny cabin, wondering whether the man was going to drag them in front of the captain or Mr. Kingsley.

To their left was a very neat bunk bed with a shelf of unintelligible books over it. The rest of the cabin was taken up with a low wide shelf which ran from the bunk to the wall. On it was a very large radio and a tray of parts. The mysterious beeping they had first heard went on and on. The man kept writing. The trapped boys looked anxiously at each other.

"Shall we go?" Simeon mouthed.

Paul nodded. Stealthily they started lifting their feet backward over the threshold. Before they were over it, the man flicked a switch on the radio, took off his headphones, and swung around on his stool. "You like radios?" he asked in very clear English, and grinned at them.

The boys lost their balance with surprise and fell at his feet.

"You must like radios!" David Yang showed them how messages were sent and received and eventually taught them the whole Morse code. "I am building a radio for my father with these parts." He pointed to the tray the boys had noticed before. "But I need another detector tube. When we get to Hong Kong I can buy it. If I can find one."

Somehow Paul and Simeon managed quite often to sneak up to David Yang's cabin during afternoon rests, and to visit different parts of the ship with him. He was like a genial older brother to them for that month on the steamer.

Days later, about an hour after we left the Hong Kong harbor, Simeon went to see if David Yang had found the radio part. He wasn't in his cabin. The second mate, a skinny little man with glasses that nearly always slipped to the end of his nose, hustled by. He couldn't speak much English and Simeon couldn't speak Cantonese, but they got along with gestures and a few words. Simeon pointed at the radio. "David Yang?" he asked, and spread his hands questioningly.

"Not?" the second mate asked, peering in, very puzzled. *"Ayah! Ayah!* Look." He nodded, pointed to himself, and hurried off, shoving his glasses up his nose.

Pretty soon the steamer slowed right down and turned around. Black smoke poured from the funnel. The *Flying Pigeon* whistled and throbbed and chugged right back into the Hong Kong harbor. Darkness fell.

"What if he's lost for good," Simeon wailed to Paul.

"Maybe he just went swimming at a nice beach."

"There's something coming."

"It's just a mast from one of those sunken ships." Paul leaned on the rail beside Simeon, his head on his arms, watching the fantastic show in the waves. The phosphorus in the water gleamed and rippled like sea lightning.

Simeon peered through the darkness toward the shore, where little lights twinkled. "Probably he got food poisoning." Several sailors straggled by, dragging some heavy manila rope.

The *Flying Pigeon* dropped anchor out in the harbor and lowered a small boat with two sailors in it who rowed for shore to hunt up the missing radio operator. About an hour later they rowed back with him.

The next morning after breakfast, when we were once again out at sea, Simeon stopped at David Yang's cabin to find out what had happened. "My friend," David Yang said, and put his hands firmly on Simeon's shoulders, "you saved me."

"What do you mean?"

"I was looking for the detector tube. My watch stopped. When I got to the dock the ship was too far out for anyone to see me. But our pay is always docked when we delay the ship. The longer the delay, the less the pay. If you hadn't found I was gone . . ." He pulled out the linings of his trousers pockets. "No pay. That would add two more years to the time until I can marry and beget my own sons." He smiled a little, as if he knew Simeon would understand the importance of sons. "If I was a regular sailor they'd just leave me behind, but I'm the only radio operator."

I think Simeon grew about a foot that day.

"Where do we go next?"

"Shanghai."

"Shanghai? Where we get off?"

"Yes."

"Oh," Simeon said, suddenly miserable. He turned and put one foot over the threshold.

David Yang laid his hand on Simeon's arm. "With letters we will stay friends."

21

As the steamer maneuvered toward the Shanghai dock, we squinted eagerly over the rail: perhaps some parents were waiting in the crowd milling around on the pier. Paul had better eyes than anyone. "What can you see, Paul?" Simeon asked.

"Well," he said slowly, craning around a pole, "I can make out a little white waving handkerchief. And there's somebody . . . important, I think, with a white uniform, and a bunch of coolies, I guess they are." He narrowed his eyes, looped his arm around the pole, and hung out a bit farther. "I can barely see a brown dog. Pretty skinny."

We groaned. I wanted to take his jug-handle ears in both my hands and use his head like a telescope. "Come on, Paul. Can you see anybody that looks like parents?"

"Nope. No parents. A truck. An empty truck. Probably for us."

It was. The truck drove us slowly through the jammed streets of Shanghai, where the wreckage of the war was plain to see: gaping holes where houses used to be, walls with the marks where rooms and stairways had been, and in the streets where everything had been leveled, there were now hastily built grass-mat shacks to house the homeless families— they looked almost like beggars' towns. I wondered about Hannah: what had she and her parents found when they got back to Germany?

The truck stopped to let several bands of soldiers past. "Mr. Kingsley," I asked, "how come there's still soldiers? I thought the war was over."

"Poor China," he answered. "Some of them are left from the world war. Some are getting ready for a civil war."

"What's a civil war?"

"Chinese against Chinese."

"I should think they'd be sick of war. Who's against who?"

"Chiang Kai-shek and the Kuomintang against Mao Tse-tung and the Communists." It sounded too complicated to think about.

On one street corner was a boy as big as Simeon, though probably quite a bit older, with straight black hair which almost covered his eyes. He crouched near a fire hydrant, with one arm crooked around a wriggly little girl. With his free hand he wet a rag at the drip of the hydrant, washed one half of her face as well as he could, then patiently held the rag under the slow drip again. A cluster of beggars watched without interest.

Slowly we rolled through the city, scattering the people, rickshaws, bikes, and carts which crowded the streets, and stopped in front of the gate of the mission compound. Inside the gate at the far end of a long path was a two-story brick building, boarded up at one end where the wall had been smashed during a bombing raid. The adult missionaries lived at that end.

Our school crowded into the other end. Wobbly black metal bunk beds were pushed so close our hair tangled in the springs, or our clothes caught and ripped, if we weren't careful. The school desks were so tight we had the feeling everyone had grown at least four elbows.

At breakfast next morning Simeon inspected the enormous cod-liver-oil capsule at his place. "I can't swallow that thing!"

"We have to. Take a swig of milk. That helps."

Simeon jerked back his elbows in an irritated gesture.

"Cut it out!" Averell said from the trestle table

behind him. "You bumped my arm and made me drop my capsule."

Simeon looked over his shoulder. They laughed, bumped noses, and turned back to the problem of the cod-liver-oil capsules.

One day a lumpy letter came. I looked closely at the large, unfamiliar writing, then squeezed it a few times. It sprang back as if something alive were inside. Simeon squeezed it. "Look!" He giggled and pointed to the curvy lines appearing on the thin air-mail paper of the envelope. "Looks like worms in that letter."

Several kids crowded over to see. "Where's it from?"

I peered at the smudgy stamp. "I think it says U.S.A. Aunt Ruth, must be."

Simeon opened his pocketknife and slowly slit the envelope. About fifty colored rubber bands jumped out—red, yellow, blue, and green.

"Luckies!"

We gathered them up, gave one to each of the kids watching, and divided the rest between us.

"But the letter. What's it say?" The others went back to their own affairs.

I read it. "Simeon, Aunt Ruth seems to think we're going to America to see her with Daddy and Mummy. D'you suppose it's true?"

A couple of months passed, broken only by our Sunday-afternoon walks through the city. Nearly every week the boy was at the fire hydrant with his little sister, trying to keep her clean.

"Look how he holds her," Anne whispered. The boy had a clever way of linking one of his arms through both of the little girl's to hold her still. "How are you, little sister?" Anne called.

The little girl stopped wriggling and stared, not trusting us. Her brother went on with his slow washing.

One Monday morning at inspection I stepped in front of Miss Elson. "Ruth, you haven't washed your face."

"I forgot."

"Look up. You forgot! Again!" She looked crossly at me, thinking. "Strapping hasn't worked. This time you'll write five hundred times, 'I must remember to wash my face in the morning.' " She handed me a thick brown pencil and a pile of rough, lined paper. Her mouth set. Her small black eyes snapped. "You should be ashamed of yourself. You've seen the boy at the hydrant?"

I nodded.

"You have all you need to make washing easy. But that poor boy . . ." She was so upset she fingered her pendant as she told how his family had all been killed during the war. He cleaned a noodle shop every day so that he and his little sister could sleep under the counter at night. The shopkeeper insisted they be clean to have that privilege.

I was ashamed. I wrote the lines, thinking about that boy. He couldn't even hope for his parents' return, but that didn't stop him from trying to take care of his little sister.

• • •

Nine more months dragged by until the Chinese celebration of the Founding of the Glorious Republic. For Anne, October 10, 1946, was the best celebration of her life: her parents came. I sat with her on the rail at the edge of the path down by the gate while she waited for them. When her parents stepped over the threshold and through the gate, she was so happy she cried, not caring who saw her. They hugged her, then held her back a little. "Four years," her dad said. "Look what four years did to our little girl!"

Next day I was sitting on the rail again doing nothing in particular, feeling pretty glum and alone, when Monica plonked herself in front of me. "What're you watching?" she asked in her busybody way.

"Nothing."

"I know," she said as if she had made a clever discovery, "you're wishing you were Anne."

"Oh, go mind your own business."

"What's the matter? What's there to make you mad about that?"

"What's . . . the matter?" I stuttered, barely able to understand her lack of understanding.

"Why are you mad?" she asked, bewildered.

"Oh, nothing." Trying to explain something so obvious to Monica, why her words irritated almost everybody, was like trying to explain how to use a screwdriver to someone who hadn't even seen a screw.

I slid off the rail and got as far from her as I could. But I *had* been wishing I were Anne. Every time we saw her for the next two days she was holding hands with either her father or her mother. Her father limped from a beam that had fallen on his leg when he was getting some children out of a bombed temple.

Just before they set sail for New Zealand, Anne and I sat on the ground leaning against the trunk of a maidenhair tree, which seemed to be the only tree on the compound to escape the bombing. She said, "Soon it will be your turn. I'm sure it will."

"How'd you know?" I mumbled.

Anne took both my hands and held them tight. "The war is over, Ruth. Remember?"

I swallowed. "I know, but I'll miss you," I said in a small gruff voice.

Her kind, round face flushed with pleasure. "You'll still have Simeon," she said. "But wait a jiff. I'll ask my dad." She said the words as if savoring them, and dashed off.

Faith, Megan, and Averell straggled by, bickering. We were all getting restless and irritable as parents arrived, a few each month, to take children away. Malcolm hurried up to them. "Do you want to help unpack the book box?"

"What book box?"

"Some Canadian Junior Red Cross kids sent us a whole crate of books!" They hurried indoors in great excitement.

I almost wished they'd sent us shoes like the last time. Mine had come from that box when we arrived in Shanghai. Already the toes had been trimmed out to make them a bit longer, but they were starting to pinch again.

After a few minutes a door slammed and Anne ran

toward me with a piece of paper in her hand. "Here. My dad says that'll get to us."

I read:

> *Anne Langdon*
> *c/o Mrs. R. Gillingham*
> *43 Raumanga Valley Road*
> *Whangarei, New Zealand.*

"Is that where those mud springs are?"

"I don't know. But I'll write and tell you if it is."

Not long after she left, Simeon and I waited with Paul on the rail near the gate. A tall, gray-haired man with tired, humped shoulders entered and Paul shaded his eyes with his hand, watching. "He's awfully thin, and his hair's gone gray, but I think that's my father," he said, and slowly slid off the rail. He stood uncertainly at the edge of the path until the man was opposite him. "Daddy?" he asked. They looked at each other like strangers straining through a mist.

"Paul!" his father exclaimed. His face, which had looked so tired and old, suddenly became much younger and full of smiles. A little shyly, Paul put his arms around him, then hid his face in his father's coat.

His mother had already gone to England with his older brothers and sisters from the concentration camp, since one sister was very sick. In a month or so their whole family would be together again in England.

A couple of days later Simeon gave Paul one of his most precious possessions, a picture postcard of

Bombay from David Yang. "You won't forget?" he asked anxiously.

Slowly Paul looked up from the card. "Hmm?"

"You won't forget . . . that you're Ratty and I'm Mole?"

"Forget! How could I forget that!" He gave Simeon a light punch in the chest. "You old duffer."

22

For almost a month Simeon and I waited. It wasn't the itchy kind of waiting. It was the kind that when you thought about it gave you a stomachache.

One day toward the end of November we sat in the schoolroom, listening to name after name, hoping for ours to be called. "Simeon and Ruth," Mr. Kingsley said with the glad little smile he always gave when letters arrived for kids who thought one would never come. He held out a smudgy envelope with about a page of stamps glued to it. We dodged the tight-packed desks to get to the front of the room. I took the thin letter, and we went slowly back to our place.

"Come on, Ruth. Open it." Simeon pushed my hand. Slowly I stuck my finger under the flap and ripped the envelope.

Dear Ruth and Simeon,

Tomorrow we will be leaving for Shanghai. Pray for a safe journey for us. We are so anxious to see both our darlings . . .

"Can you believe it's really happening?" I asked Simeon. But he'd laid his head on his arms, covering his face.

I got ready to read the next part, but the words were so awful I licked my thumb and smeared the ink. It said, "We've tried to tell Benjamin about you but he can't quite understand." What a terrible monster he must be, I thought, not even to understand about his own brother and sister. I wished they'd leave him behind.

The rest of the letter was all right. It told about the housing and food they were arranging for some of the Chinese who had lost everything in the war, including people from their own families.

Two weeks of thick gray clouds passed, clouds which made you want to take a huge scraper and push them back, simply to see if the sun was still there. At the end of the second week it poured rain. The next day the sun shone, for us, Simeon and I thought. This was our mother and father's coming-day.

We sat on the rail down by the great gate. "It may be a while," we were cautioned. But we didn't care. We'd sit there all day if we had to.

"*Wei! Wei! Wei!*" somebody yelled, and banged on the outside of the gate.

The gatekeeper shuffled to the door. "Have patience. Have patience," he hollered.

"I wait," the voice from the street answered. Simeon and I craned forward, clinging to the rail, our eyes on the crack.

Slowly the gatekeeper opened the door. A bald-headed coolie struggled through with a shoulder yoke, carrying baskets of potatoes and cabbages. We watched him trot all the way up the path and around to the side of the building. Simeon began to wriggle.

"Home free!" somebody called from the other side of the building.

"*Wei! Wei!*" Another shout from the street. More banging. This sounded important. Maybe? Simeon and I looked at each other for a few seconds, as if a word might break the magic. The gatekeeper pulled at his thin little beard, grumblingly pushed himself off his low bamboo stool, and again shuffled to the door and slid back the bolt. A Chinese man, an evangelist maybe, stepped up over the high threshold, followed by a couple of tattered soldiers who stumbled. They talked a few minutes with the gatekeeper, who grumpily pointed to a side door. The evangelist walked smartly up the path followed by the two scared soldiers, who glanced suspiciously at us. We smiled and they looked very surprised.

"Eighty-nine, ninety, ninety-one . . ." came faintly to our ears from the hide-and-seek game.

Simeon almost fell off the rail, he was getting so wriggly. "Why don't you go inside? They won't come. Not yet they won't come." He looked helplessly at me, then dashed in to the toilet.

Just as the door slammed, the gatekeeper went muttering and fussing to answer another shout. I clutched the rail. A European man stepped through, carrying a black suitcase, followed by two women holding wicker cases. They stopped near the gatekeeper's stool as if waiting for somebody else to come.

The gatekeeper craned through the door, looking

down the street, then drew back, muttering. A tired-looking woman with curly gray hair carrying a blue cloth bag nearly tripped as she stepped up over the threshold. I leaned forward, gripping the rail more tightly. She was our mother! Our father steadied her with his free hand. In his other arm he carried the monster-baby, who wasn't a monster at all. Benjamin was perfect: round and rosy and curly.

"Daddy! Mummy!" I yelled, but they just glanced toward me and walked on up the path. My insides felt dumped out. Had I been that bad? Had I disappointed them so utterly? Maybe God was punishing me for all the bad things I'd done. My eyes stuck to their backs. Then Simeon came hurtling down the path and jumped into our mother's arms, hugging her tight as tight. I wished the night would hurry and eat me up.

Suddenly our father stopped. He turned around and put the baby down on the path. Benjamin howled, grabbed our mother's leg, and hung on for dear life. But our father strode toward me as if he'd seen something just beyond me. "Oh, Ruthie girl, Ruthie girl." He put his arms around me. "It's been so long and you've grown so big we didn't even know our own little girl." I felt tears on the back of my neck. I was so glad I could hardly breathe.

That night, for a treat, we were allowed to sit up late on the bed in our parents' cramped room. A crib was set up at the foot of the bed, but Benjamin wasn't interested in sleeping there. He crawled all over our laps, then stood teetering in the middle of the bed and clapped for himself. "Wonder! Wonder!" he cheered.

"He's just learned to walk," our mother said, and gave him her finger to keep him from toppling over. "He was sick so much at first, he was a little slow developing."

I asked, "Why did you say he was a monster with a fat tongue that hung out and giant teeth?"

Our mother looked at our father, both very perplexed. "When did we say that, snookie?"

"In the letter about his being born."

"Can you remember anything else in the letter?"

I told what I could. "There were lots of censor holes, too, so I got mixed up."

Our father frowned and scratched the back of his head. Then his face cleared. "That must have been when those two Flying Tigers took us out to see their crashed plane painted like a tiger shark."

"Did you really think he was so deformed?" our mother asked.

I nodded. "I thought—"

"Ruthie. Simmy," Benjamin interrupted, and put his fat little hands in mine.

"He said our names! He does know us!" I pulled him into my lap, where he stayed for about half a minute.

We started talking about remembering: Hongen, our amah, the mulberry tree, the bicycle shop. That set Simeon off talking about the steamer.

"I think I'll be a ship's radio operator when I grow up. Paul and I practiced Morse code." He took the fountain pen and an envelope from our father's shirt pocket and wrote ...−−−... "That means 'save our souls,' and I know lots more." He looked enormously pleased with himself.

Benjamin fell asleep in the middle of the bed like a little fat bird in a very full nest.

"Oh, I almost forgot. I've got a present for Mummy. I've kept it ever so long." Simeon dug in his pocket, then passed her something folded in a piece of torn sheet. She started opening it. "Hold it up to the light," he commanded.

"That's beautiful! Where did you get it?"

"It's moonstone. See the new moon shape?" He told about the pigeons in Kunming.

We filled that small room with us and our glad talking.

Then our father said, "Well, Simeon old fellow, did Ruthie take good care of you?" I felt kicked in the stomach. I stopped jiggling the bed and stared down at the ink smudge that never came off my writing finger. Now Simeon can get back for all the times I was mean to him, I thought.

I heard him take a deep breath and flop back in our mother's lap. "Yep." His voice was glad, but he was quiet for a few minutes. "She didn't let me get lost and she . . ." By the time he was through, I could have hugged him so tight my arms would have broken around him.

I lifted my head to look at our mother and father. Their eyes shone. "We're proud of our big girl."

Gladness came right from the ends of my nails, and filled me so full I could only give a huge, happy sigh. Thanks be to God, I thought, for a little while there'll be no war or boarding school or trying to take care of Simeon; instead, a long holiday with our mother and father visiting aunts and uncles and cousins in England and in America.